"Imagine a modern Don Juan playing the lead in *Women in Love*, directed by Nabokov with lyrics by Cole Porter, and you'll have a rough—if somewhat overblown—estimate of *A Presence with Secrets*.... Spackman drenches these dalliances in laughter and light. . . . On finishing *A Presence with Secrets*, I turned right back to page one to read it again."   —*Newsweek*

"A marvelous novel by an extraordinarily gifted writer."
                                                             —*Virginia Quarterly Review*

"[A] style that Henry James might have risen to if he possessed sexuality and a sense of humor."   —J.D. O'HARA, *New England Review*

"Reading *A Presence with Secrets* is like taking a warm bath in luxurious prose style."   —*Boston Globe*

"W. M. Spackman is one of our great writers. Like Henry Green and Laurence Sterne, he is a storyteller, a comic, an enchanter, but first and foremost a master stylist; the magic of his books arises from the eccentric elegance of his sentences. . . . A masterpiece."   —*Soho News*

Also by W. M. Spackman

HEYDAY

ON THE DECAY OF HUMANISM
(*Essays*)

AN ARMFUL OF WARM GIRL

A
PRESENCE
WITH
SECRETS

by W. M. Spackman

A Dutton **Obelisk** Paperback

E. P. DUTTON, INC. | NEW YORK

This paperback edition of *A Presence with Secrets* first published in 1982
by E. P. Dutton

Edmund White's introduction first appeared in the *Village Voice*

Published in the United States by
E. P. Dutton, Inc.
2 Park Avenue, New York, N.Y. 10016

Library of Congress Catalog Card Number: 82-72044

ISBN: 0-525-48022-6

Published simultaneously in Canada by
Clarke, Irwin & Company Limited, Toronto and Vancouver

10 9 8 7 6 5 4 3 2 1

To
Laurice
Present
and
Future

INTRODUCTION

by Edmund White

To write decent English prose, to have a style, or, better yet, an ear—that seems a hopeless ambition at times. Just as one cannot step outside one's own aesthetic values and declare, "I have no taste at all," (except as a philistine boast or an angling for compliments), in the same way a writer cannot logically complain about his own prose. If he knew better he'd write better.

And yet writers do worry about style and quarrel about it and squirrel away bits of literary wisdom. I could catalogue rather quickly my own poor accumulation, at least the books I've put together out of this century: Ezra Pound's prose and poetry; Fowler's *Guide to Modern English Usage*; Plomer's *The Diamond of Jannina*; the poems of Elizabeth Bishop and James Merrill; and the fiction of Ronald Firbank, Henry Green, Vladimir Nabokov, William Burroughs, Coleman Dowell—and now W. M. Spackman.

For anyone who aspires to a style that can wheel dramatically close to its subject for a pore-by-pore inspection, then track inexorably through the parting dancers or place an unsmudged glass before a window silver with sunstruck rain; for anyone eager to write a single sentence that holds in suspension particles of wisdom and nonsense, action and observation, lust and loveliness; for anyone who is curious about the verbal art of picturing things and maneuvering a reader, as distinct from such less elusive aspects of fiction as plot, suspense, symbolism, and "message"; for this dwindling but avid crew of devotees, Spackman's new novel *A Presence with Secrets* will come as a great clarification. It is the most stylish, vital, and worldly book to emerge—well, since his last book, *An Armful of Warm Girl*.

The style owes a debt to both Henry Green and Ivy Compton-Burnett. It was Green (inspired in turn by Charles M. Doughty's *Travels in Arabia Deserta*) who devised a written language that strikes us as "artificial" only because it approximates the flexibility, the concreteness, and surprising syntax of spoken English. We like to assure ourselves that no distinction exists in English between spoken demotic and written hieratic and that our literature has no need of a Raymond Queneau, who so regularly distressed and delighted his readers with shocking phoneticizations of the French they were speaking every day. But in fact there *is* a gap in English (and American) so great that we can't hear the quaint music, the oddly placed stress in many sentences in Green or Spackman unless we say them out loud.

I'm not suggesting that Green or Spackman chart the trackless wastes of ordinary chatter or render its mindlessness and feeble energy. Quite the contrary. These writers have contrived a literary manner that is hard, condensed, often epigrammatic, but that does draw for its effects on the repetitions of speech, the gliding elisions, its illogical leaps, inversions—the stuttering of thought and feeling. Here's a paragraph from Green's *Loving*:

"They were wheeling wheeling in each other's arms heedless at the far end where they had drawn up one of the white blinds. Above from a rather low ceiling five great chandeliers swept one after the other almost to the waxed parquet floor reflecting in their hundred thousand drops the single sparkle of distant day, again and again red velvet panelled walls, and two girls, minute in purple, dancing multiplied to eternity in these trembling pears of glass."

It can be equaled by this description in Spackman—or rather exceeded, since Spackman's syntax is itself a crystal drop, shattering and multiplying the image seen through it:

"He got to his feet and turned uneasily to the room. Whose vaults of darkness were now filling he saw with the hearth's reanimated crimsons again, corners emerging, murmurous with soft dusk; and as if from aisles of twilight the bed loomed out now before him palely luminous, night gone from its tall canopies, through which the coals' fluttering images were cast so faint in under that where the girl lay he could not make out for sure, thickets of shadow were so dense, only the folds of the bed's hangings fell fire-dyed, damasks and wavering vermilions, and in the brocade of its swags glints of dull gold."

From Compton-Burnett, Spackman has learned how to pay unblinking attention to the balletic intricacies of refined small talk, conversation that epitomizes her novels and his with its emphasis on originality of presentation and perfect conventionality of subject. There are also differences.

In Spackman the conversations occur less often, are generally reported in indirect discourse, and the speakers are less penetrating, less bourgeois-smug, more hectic and bewitching, as in these lines from *An Armful of Warm Girl*:

"He shouted into the phone, 'Good god Victoria do you seriously pretend to think with one lovely melting melted atom of you that a single atom of me will ever forget anything about you till the day the last breath sighs out of my body?'

She said in moved tones, 'Such a rhetorical liar, oh Nicholas.'"

The temptation to fill up my pages with quotations from Spackman attests to his accomplishment. He has done away with tiresome exposition at the outset and philosophical musing for the wrap-up. There is no merely mechanical filling in of obligatory scenes, no unsavory ponderings of the meaning of events, no throat-clearings, no characters nor situations foreign to his understanding or ungrateful to his talent. Like the first painter who realized he could do away with the holy family and concentrate on the landscape or eliminate the diners and render the peaches and napery, Spackman has stripped away everything irrelevant to his genius. He seems the sort of artist who makes his decisions by depending on goose-bumps. The things that galvanize him are women, adultery, French food and wine (the menus are explicit and astounding), the sound of laughing lovers calling to each other in a darkened house, the tricks light plays on a mirror, slyly elegant nonsense, the adherence to old codes of behavior, not least of all an etiquette of sexual civility as golden and noble as a departing couple in a painting by Watteau. These are his subjects, as is the feeling of transience that must shadow so much pleasure.

Although Spackman was born in 1905, he has written only four books: a novel, *Heyday* (1953); a collection of critical essays, *On the Decay of Humanism* (1967); and two recent novels, both published by Knopf, *An Armful of Warm Girl* (1978) and *A Presence with Secrets* (1980). Rumor has it that he's now hard at work on his own version of Henry James's *The Ambassadors*, the book with the thrilling *donnee* and too little worldliness to work it out; if we are to rely on Spackman's essay on James, he considers the master to have been one of the most uneven writers of all time. As he concludes in a great stinging overkill of a peroration: "In James, all is unconsidered paradox and confusion of the will—a constant self-exhortation to 'dramatize, dramatize!' yet a devotion to a way of writing that slows the action to a crawl and inundates the plot with a bilge of irrelevances; an infatuation with mechanical melodrama and well-made boulevard play, yet an unwillingness to work out his scenes a faire to the full; overanxiety about his audience, yet delusions of what it consisted of and blindness to what his lamentable anxiety implied; creativity confounded with the mere scrabble of industriousness; above all, the arrogance of a settled way."

If judged by his own standards, Spackman receives high marks; he's certainly not guilty of "the arrogance of a settled way." His first novel,

Heyday, is packed with incidents and characters and covers many years, a capaciousness he will reject in the later two novels. The tone of *Heyday* is an unsettling mixture of the factual and the fabulous. We must work our way through circumstantial accounts of court trials, job prospects, money troubles, and infidelities-in-the-interest-of-career, in order to arrive at those magical passages that seem the pale sapphires in overly busy mounts—the nostalgic visit to Wilmington, for instance, or a tete-a-tete luncheon of martinis for him, whiskey sours for her, pure pleasure for us. And the voices of the young women—they have the authentic Spackman ring of well-bred strategic vagueness. These are voices we'll be hearing again.

The Decay of Humanism (published by Rutgers) is the sort of confident display of erudition and high-handed opinion we learned to expect from Nabokov—the table talk of someone who knows he's a genius. When it was brought out, Spackman had published only the one novel, and yet his language reveals that faint archaic smile of the author of a masterpiece (indeed, he'd already written one, *An Armful of Warm Girl,* but 15 publishers had rejected it and he was to shelve it for two decades). In *The Decay of Humanism* Spackman, who taught Classics for years, is able to say of Aristotle's *Poetics,* "Of what earthly use to the critic or the writer is a dissection of literature by a marine biologist?"

Everyone may love a good Aristotelean yarn—indeed the devising of plot may be central to the poetics of prose—but the truth is that in contemporary fiction the most interesting "action" occurs from sentence to sentence, word to word. The energy generated by a contemporary book is sparked by the way the story unfolds through a particular sensibility—the art of brilliant fragments or what used to be called the "decadent" style before Richard Gilman removed that word from any sensible writer's vocabulary. Or one might say that what's exciting in new novels is what cannot be filmed—the rendering of the scenes as apart from the simple anecdote.

In *A Presence with Secrets,* Spackman has reduced the anecdote to its simplest elements in order to give himself room for the delights of rendering; just as Morandi chose to paint nothing but bottles, Spackman has restricted himself to romance. But the love he portrays is not the sort we're used to reading about. In most bourgeois novels (most novels, that is), the love is hopeless, one-sided, doomed from the start; if the love is to flower at all, it must do so by virtue of a miracle, since the lovers come from different classes, races, from warring families or warring nations, and so on. The handsome man marries the homely woman, the child and the old lady become lovers, the races mingle and the classes merge. In life people are far less romantic, far more practical and predictable. In fact a cynic might say that the *function* of romantic fiction is to persuade readers that sincerity and inner beauty can transcend class barriers, just as the lottery suggests that chance can erase poverty.

In Spackman's novels the lovers do not reach for each other across a social chasm. The romances do not dramatize large social conflicts nor produce an illusory solution to real tensions. Instead, the lovers are all privileged and physically beautiful. Moreover, they all subscribe to the same code: that the institution of marriage is unlikely to house for long such a bird of passage as passion; that passion itself is not brutal or even primarily biological but rather tender and civil; that the only way to survive the sadness of living and loving is with a reckless gaiety of spirit. Spackman's men and women are all co-conspirators, libertines willing to propitiate the deities of convention in order to secure the joys of dalliance. Spackman's lovers do not suffer. Whereas most fictional lovers suffer, I'd say, in an *exemplary* way (their torments are emblems or scaled-down versions of society's inequities), Spackman's characters reveal what people feel when love is free, uncoded. These feelings turn out to be sweetness, sensuality, loneliness, and an amazement at the appalling otherness of others. Which is what the title means; another person, one's lover, is a presence with secrets.

The novel is divided into three sections. In the first Hugh Tatnall, a painter from Philadelphia and a veteran rake, is in bed with a frightened young American innocent doing her junior year abroad. She and he, who've barely known one another till now, have been caught in an outbreak of mob violence in Florence and found shelter in a *pensione*. As the girl sleeps, no longer innocent, Hugh worries about the whereabouts of his Anglo-Irish mistress, who has vanished in the political chaos. When the girl awakens and quizzes the much older Hugh about love and sex and how they strike a man, he tells her that "making love was always it seemed somehow new and unexpected, and who you made love with always this stranger, always new, this lovely phoenix. Which was why making love he said, stroking her, was an exploration he did not see how he or any man could ever come to an end of or want to—here was this Being in your bed, this secret presence, and what could you feel you'd ever want more on earth than to discover who she was, this charming stranger."

In the second section, Hugh's cousin, a Main Line divorcee, tells us of her affair with the willing man—and of their visit to a French vicomte's chateau in Brittany, where they are suddenly held at gun point by working-class thugs. When the thugs leave, the three upper-class characters luxuriate in their privacy: "And then for a moment, it was no more than a wordless breath of time, the three of us sat there in one of those strange soft silences, like a transition between two worlds—as if from the tone one talks in when there are people there who aren't like us, to how we talk when there aren't. I mean we are brought up to say things in ways such people will understand, it saves time. And, really, their feelings I expect too. Because with them we *say* instead of just half-say with implications and references taken for granted that would make them see they were left out, anyhow now here was this sudden little silence, and I said to myself we are all three en pays de connaissance and thinking the same things about these men but won't say so, and this what the silence is about."

Like many writers (Shakespeare, for instance), Spackman makes birth a condition for civility, but any time at all spent with the actual rich or well-bred convinces the reader that Spackman's vision is utopian, a glimpse of what people, freed from poverty and ignorance, might become. Yet even in such an Edenic state, people will remain pregnant with secrets. As the narrator tells us, "even a lover is an ally against loneliness who still hasn't claim enough to encroach upon my solitude for me 'to know.'" If the beloved is a shifting field of secrets, a pulsing solitude, the dead are a cold and static enigma—and in the final section of the novel Hugh's friends and lovers gather around his coffin (he's been murdered by a lesbian rival).

Of course, if solitude is accepted, measured, cherished, and if the inevitable distance between two people is turned from desolation into coquetry, then life regains it enchantment and becomes once more practicable—or at least endurable. The closing lines of *A Presence with Secrets* confirms this optimism:

"'Sweet Simon,' she said, sliding a gloved hand through my arm, 'you can't *still* be surprised!'

"So, as I recall it, I answered, 'Always'—enchantment being (with luck) what it can sometimes turn out to be."

But of course that is what art—or at least Spackman's art—surely must be, the very distillation of enchantment, the consolation for life.

CONTENTS

A
PRESENCE
WITH
SECRETS

". . . and, well, *shy*, then!" she said in her haughtiest clear young voice and not looking even near him in the rosy fire-flowered darkness, speaking in fact less to this lover just acquired than to the bed's dusky canopies, or to the soaring Renaissance night of the ceiling where now the hearth's reflected images breathed their tumbled and disintegrating crimsons—a Miss Rosemary Decazalet by name, abed as it happened in Firenze, on a night of tumult and deep spring, a properly brought up girl for any reasonable purpose including this one, and in any case, and already, as good as twenty years old.

So in the hooded Giotto bed, ". . . feeling shy," she mumbled, lolling her pretty head down into the deepest pillows away from him, folding her legs chidingly aside and aloof on their tender hinge, in fact half turning her charming young back on him, wanting suddenly very much, as it seemed, to hide.

So in a kindly way he was amused.

But having been so humbly kissed there by that soft young mouth, who could think of smiling at the child? so although she was not looking at him, still he made his face show a gentlemanly concern.

Also he was a good deal embarrassed at what he had let happen.

For they had not taken refuge in this elegant room to make love good god! but in a hairsbreadth run for it out of the path of that headlong mob suddenly from nowhere on their very heels—though then it had hurtled past and on, toward the questura it may have been, the narrow quattrocento street such a tossing flood of packed and racing bodies the powdery old walls you felt shook with the weight catapulting along past them and on, so at the last moment he'd as good as flung her out from under its impact, aside, into the courtyard of this pensione or whatever it was, gasping. And *shaken*, by god! Then he'd seen she was white with terror, even going faint, so he'd banged on the door. And had the padrona give them a room for her for a bit, and had brandy sent up.

Casa d'appuntamenti though he very shortly saw (and now, with irony) the place must be.

But *this* to have happened!—and when this angel beside him he'd known little more than to say buon giorno to: a conversazione evening or two at the Fonteviots', a tea at the British circolo. Even this time merely happened on her, she was window-shopping in the Vicolo del Forno and it was absolute chance, he'd no more than been taking that way back from the Lungarno. Then, and there had been no warning to them whatever, a distant shout or two but in Italy what was that, they were standing chatting, she was asking deferential questions about his portrait of Mrs. Fonteviot, when suddenly up at the far end of the vicolo that wild scattering of people running, slipping on the smooth old cobbles and one man had gone down, and next instant this massive rolling wall of mob swept round the corner with the speed of a tide-bore right over the fellow and down upon *them*.

So no wonder the brandy, when that sleek padrona brought it, the girl had near spilled with trembling. Eyes enormous; and her teeth had chattered so against the shivering glass he'd had to take it from her cold fingers and hold it for her, steady, and get sips into her between shuddering sobs.

Because *nothing* like this had she conceived could happen before her eyes *ever* or she be so terrified, she told him chokingly—for what was *happening*, could it even be did he think the end of not the world perhaps but the whole government? for oh this *was* how revolutions began, with awful murderous mobs like that, how could he say they didn't? And that poor man who'd stumbled and fallen had been *trampled to death* hadn't he? Before their *eyes!*

So he had been a good long time lulling her.

Till, then, finally, well, the end of the world was what finally she'd behaved as if she thought it was, and no tomorrow.

And now was overcome at herself.

—He saw therefore he had to be wary for a while about how he put things.

For about this child he knew nothing. It was unpredictable. They can go he knew flutteringly shy at being seen in a bath yet be in tears if you misguidedly didn't; and there, it is only about vanity. Here it could be about anything. So he was silent. He did not see what a man of sense could risk unless she said more.

But she was now it seemed too humbled to say anything, indeed in that warm fire-hung darkness her body's tender arabesques he thought drew farther, if anything, away from him and apart, in upon themselves, so that he saw the slender buckling curve of waist and back he could paint with a delight as deep as only just now had plundered his senses. But he also thought that if for the moment he should touch her it was unpredictable.

So for the moment he let it go.

In any case, staying on, as now arranged, by morning he might have decently seen to it she was left unhumiliated. For otherwise it was too heartless.

Also, as he'd said to that padrona when he'd gone down to say they'd stay, why risk making it back to his own quarter of the city on a night of carnage like this?—running battles in the streets if nothing deadlier, non finivano mai, questi baccani!

Ma come, "baccani"! Was a *nothing* (she humored him,

Etruscan eyes dark with innuendo)—un pochino di baruffa municipale, the signore needn't—

Call it a little fuss or what she liked, he said, the young lady'd been *badly* upset by it. Still was, in fact.

Ma se conviene al signore—

Thank 'ee yes, he'd said blandly, suit him it would; so they'd stay on. And he'd want a little dinner sent up to them shortly, too; something light if she'd have the kindness to manage it?

Though as to any dinner—that had turned out not to be what he'd gone back up for, the complicities of a kindly Iddio being what sometimes they were. He lay and looked at this unexpected blessing of his, and in the luxury of it, almost yawned.

But suddenly in the night outside, and from so near by somewhere that right under their windows it sounded, this shocking cry, half a scream, and in an instant the child had uncoiled up out of her pillows like a spring, eyes enormous again into his, wordlessly imploring, and just then along the house wall below feet went racketing past, frantic, and with a little stricken sound she sat bolt upright, the hearth's now faltering and shadowy crimsons staining every madonna slope of throat and breast, or as if she were strewn deep in those dying roses, spray upon spray, so that before she'd clutched the coverlet childishly up he thought once more what a lovely bribe to have Iddio (or Whoever) simply hand him like this, which however anybody can of course be indulged with now and then who knows why, but what sheer blazing luck from Heaven it is, what a blessing, when they do.

Still, to reassure her, he groped to the window; though when he slung the heavy satins of the curtain aside he made out whoever it had been was gone.

All beyond was in deep darkness, under he saw thick mist above, night-glow from the luminous city around them thrown up saffron against filmy overcast, to be drawn in there, under great lifting curtains and pale coils of cloud, so that light was shed back down too faint anywhere, he hardly made out what this window gave on, below, muffled in black geometries of shadow; a small private square it seemed. And even elegant, a seicento façade over across, arcaded and ornate, the galleria a run of rounded arches all along it, also what must be the shape of a fountain, some spouting nymph he supposed, or riding marble waves a boy and dolphin, anyhow he heard the cold splash of water on stone. Silence again too everywhere, only damp breaths of night-sound rising like exhalations from dark streets and squares, where at last it smelt of spring.

So ecco, he said over his shoulder, in reassurance, and let the long folds of the curtain swing down straight again—there was nothing; had been nothing; late-night passanti scuffling. In any case not that rabble they'd run into, or anything like. But this without looking round at her, for he thought fright, yes, but also the delicate point now was, more likely, how with kindness to get her over what she was so stricken had happened, this helpless shock at herself he supposed: trouble with innocence was historical perspective, it had still to learn what was praxis. So, first, then, deal also with this woebegone nudity. Engaging or not.

There should be the usual toweling vestaglie warming on pipes in the bathroom. Where when he went to look there of course were. So he draped himself in one and brought her the other, saying amiably, here, put this round her pretty shoulders, she couldn't spend her life under these comic European eiderdowns could she? while he saw to the fire.

On whose incandescent hummocks of ember he took his time shaking from the scuttle dribblings of fresh coal. Culm, it appeared: soft dusts kindled instantly, showering sparks, then soon the whole hearth glowed again, strewing its roses deep into the room's vaults of shadow, so that when he turned round at last and found great innocent eyes dolefully upon him, those crimsons fluttering in her cheek anyone would have taken for hopeless blushing, so deep among the bed's canopies of night had the hearth distributed its insubstantial emblems.

And blushing she may have been—helplessly not even he supposed being sure merely what next, or expected to know, for in the fire-fringed shadows she dropped her eyes from his to her cold hands. It seemed she could not speak for misery. Or gêne, for he saw it might be she had no idea what in this situation a girl found—desperately, or even at all—to say. A topic, even. Or, generally, what was, well, *expected!*

This unforeseen . . . could he label it "threshold-ritual"? anthropologically speaking it had been gone through like an angel, but on from there is not so near second nature. Including light drawing-room conversation if called for.

So, humanely, and still from across the room, imagine, he said to her (as if in complaint), getting caught in another of these pointless Mediterranean revolutions, what a damn' nuisance. Assuming revolution was actually what it was, for he said genially he hardly thought Italy, Firenze anyhow, was a place any practical-minded Marxist would pick to start one. With *their* millennial history of total political cynicism? *And* all the black-marketable antiquities!

But she said in a shamed voice, "I thought we were going to die."

Yes, well, after a moment he conceded, he supposed it was mostly that ominous lowering sound of a mob coming, like a typhoon. It *was* daunting; daunted anybody. So in pure primitive reflex people turned and ran.

Whereas she'd seen for herself all they'd really needed to do, she and he, was step into the nearest doorway, or a courtyard, or anywhere out of the way. He was appalled he'd frightened her by not doing that on the spot. Instead of haring off first like a fool—luxurious as this pensione (or whatever it was) had in the event turned out to be.

But still it seemed she could not look at him, it was such a hopelessness, only murmuring something downcast about

". . . una condotta di collegio . . ." as if she did not see how, in English, she could possibly ever bring herself to face such a thing.

"Boarding-school behavior" he thought was one libel it was not!—when was this woebegone angel going to divagate back into sense?

But he asked her, coaxing, trying though not to sound kindly—asked her what on earth made anyone as lovely as she was think she had to take refuge (or whatever) in Italian? And from what!

Stunned still, he thought, looking at her, by that mob. The sheer sundering momentum of it is what stuns—the huge rolling weight of this one like an immense wave flung in along the seawall of some narrow shod of a bay, to burst in its thunders on the drowned stones of the quay; the earth's foundations seem to shake; and so no wonder if even now perhaps she was in dread, these walls ready in her mind to reel and fall.

So dammit he said was she perversely trying to make *him* wretched with regret, compunction rather, over what had happened?—when there wasn't an atom of his body not in a kind of wonder at what her sweetness had blessed him with!

This rather over-worldly rhetoric at least got her eyes back to him, though still she seemed too uncertain what to say next to speak.

To give her time, then, he went to the wine-bucket for what might be left. And a good half bottle was; he was surprised. So he poured and brought her her glass and at any rate she took it.

He therefore risked settling on a chaste corner of the bed with his own glass. And brought the bottle along.

For he said look, he knew she sounded as if she wanted him to explain her to herself but did he really need to? As wouldn't she consent to see? He meant she didn't need *him* to tell her how lovely she was, did she? And meantime the wine in that glass in her hand was there to be drunk: beautifully cold, and as moelleux a white Hermitage as he ever remembered tasting outside France, a pleasure to happen on.

So at least she meekly raised the glass to her lips and sipped a little, great rueful eyes seeming now to plead.

Having still, though, no real idea what to say, he was continuing more or less rhetorically, had she no sense of what between one heartbeat and the next sometimes—when she decided to explain.

Viz., "But this—this— What I— Well, *this!*" in a little wail of woe.

In fact as good as reproaching him.

"And when don't you see I'd never so much as called you by your first *name* even, before I simply— Oh *how could I!*" she mourned. "And it wasn't even partly your fault!" she accused him, choking.

The answer to this hardly being that he'd never happened to call her anything but Miss Decazalet either, and a mere couple of times at that, he had for the moment no idea what form of reassurance he could fall back on to comfort her with.

But she said in a sad little voice, "Because when you're so famous how was I to think of you except that way," as if making sense.

He said, amused, "But how did—"

"Well but aren't you?" she cried. "You're a terribly famous painter—you *are*, there was a part of a whole *lecture* in our art-department moderns course on you! And even here you're 'il Tatnall'! So when you came into Mrs. Fonteviot's salotto that first time—I mean how could I possibly think I'd ever be like *this* with you," she entreated him. "Even if Mrs. Fonteviot did laugh and say goodness should she risk introducing a girl her godmother had put in her charge to a painter who—who made even a still life look as if—"

Yes, yes, he said, and laughed, that was Alex's standard epigram about him—an elegant creature, Mrs. Fonteviot, but she couldn't it seemed tell him from Courbet! And the English upper classes did go in for low language, earls' daughters and other ladyships it sometimes seemed in particular.

"Well, but," the child said in a diffident voice, "that wonderful whoever-she-was of yours in the National Gallery sort of does look ..."

Camilla?—good god he said what a nonsense, he'd posed her in the exact posture of Michelangelo's Erythrean Sibyl! why, what on earth, he said agreeably, did she think the picture was about?

So, not knowing, she was silent.

Or anyhow for a moment, before gently conceding, "Well of course then I found you were charming *too*, I mean I saw you at evening parties, and that time at the circolo, and you were terribly nice to me, anyhow I thought you were. But that could have been I knew because of Mrs. Fonteviot and good manners. Anyway I'm not—I just don't have the mondanità for *this*," she said humbly, "because anyway all I thought was what it would be like to know you well. And what you might feel about me if I did, being famous. But now even after *this* I don't know!" she cried at him in a sudden little fume. "I might no more than have just met you! And then to *go to bed* with you!"

And before he could answer a word mumbled, "When I haven't said your first name even *yet* ..." in a voice of tears.

—All of which anyone could see was leading nowhere.

In mere humanity therefore he moved up toward her, set the Hermitage and his glass too on the table de chevet, sat down again on the edge of the shadowy bed a respectful six inches from the nearest part of this mournful child, and said oh now now now.

This maneuver however only made her look at him a little wildly, eyes wide with new misgivings.

So he slid a hand, palm up and harmless, under hers that lay on the coverlet there between them; and when after a quivering moment she seemed to nerve herself to look down at this piece of unseduction (though what more innocent could any man do?) he let his fingertips slip their blameless way an inch or so farther, to where the pulse beat in her soft wrist, which they caressed as if in affection or simple cajolery, there in the smooth folds of her sleeve; though otherwise for a space the two of them were as motionless there as amanti in some sepulchral marble, among tombs.

Till finally she swallowed and murmured, ". . . Well, *Hugh*, then" in a sheepish voice, and looked at him, placating. Though she drew her hand away.

And, also, complained gently, "Except Hugh you do see how I did have to feel, I mean how am I to think you really feel anything about me, don't you see? When the way I've behaved—And I know you think being upset is just silly! And anyway it *is*, isn't it! And after all the girls who must've made —who've been in love with you!"

Now now, she needn't make him sound, he said, like some damn' pasha!—and a pasha at the end of a long and well-supplied life, at that.

Or was she just saying (as near as good manners would let her) that he was too old for her, he asked amiably.

"Why, you're not old!" she cried, astonished at him. "But you can't be! I mean, how old are you?"

Thirty-seven he told her next birthday.

"But Hugh, that isn't *old!*"

Old enough to've conducted himself with more regard for the ordinary amenities than he had, he said he thought was pretty obvious. To have upset an angel like her like this? A certain disinvoltura was all very well and expected, but not as unthinkingly as this! Here, give him her glass, at least he could see to that properly.

So as if bemused by this, in wonder, she watched him pour. And pour into his own glass and set the bottle down, in silence. Till at last she said in a meek voice, "Yes only Hugh because I was so frightened and silly doesn't mean I still didn't feel about you as if—"

Frightened and silly if she liked, yes, he said, but was he at his age to be innocent of eventualities?—what could happen he meant too often did.

". . . But I let it," she said, looking down at her glass.

So after a moment therefore he slid his hand under hers again. And said as if conversationally yes but the *point* was, and she must have been aware of it, from that first time in Alex's salotto he'd thought what a lovely thing she was—hardly meant for him he meant, but what painter in his senses wouldn't have? But dammit making love was not something to be done "all'improvvisto"! and what reason had he had to imagine she'd even had occasion to think about him? Much more do anything like make up her mind about him if she had, in short what he was saying was that he was dismayed at himself.

"Oh, *thought* about you, yes! I don't see how you could expect any girl— Why, but you're lllllovely!" she laughed, exulting. "It was just, well, *how* it happened, Hugh, I mean 'improvvisto' sounds so horrid!"

But wasn't when it wasn't, he said amiably, and picking up her hand turned it palm up and put his lips to the inside of her sweet young wrist.

"Oh Hugh. Oh *dear* this is all so hard on my objectivity! Only don't let's talk Italian. I know I was, but I felt shy. No but d'you know what's surprising?"

Nothing so surprising he said about feeling shy.

"But surprising about making *love*, silly! It's how sort of devoted to you it seems to make me feel about you afterwards, is surprising."

What flattery, he said, smiling.

"Am I? I mean aren't you supposed to deserve it?" she asked, smiling too. "It's just that it isn't what you hear makes you expect you'll feel, somehow, is all."

But he said didn't even *her* rather offhand generation occasionally—

"Oh well at *school*," she said, coolly pitying this, for how immature. "At school of course everybody says it seems to be a sheer toss-up what it's like, it's with just boys. Anyway," she murmured, "not like *this*, Hugh—oh my!"

So then she didn't really need, did she (he asked, and in fact what could have been more reasonable) *didn't* need to be upset any more about it surely at all? What was there to gaze at him with those great doubtful eyes about?

"Yes except *then*, Hugh, I hadn't— I mean it was because I was so beside myself."

But good god what had that to do with it? he protested, as if this were true, setting his glass on the table de chevet (and hers out of the way there too, come to think of it) for he *swore* to her—

"But if I made love with you now," she said in an uncertain voice, "I mean *again*, how could I ever, well, explain it to myself later? I don't mean it isn't that I don't feel—that you're not terribly— Oh well oh *dear!*" she ended dolefully, for he had taken both her hands.

And saying couldn't she see for herself that six inches was a senseless distance now between them anyhow? kissed her submissive mouth at last; and though she whispered as if in gentle despair, aux abois, lost, "Are you my love? . . ." in the warm hearth-lit shadows of their bed she collapsed obediently into his arms.

—It might therefore have been hardly an hour, but however long, for in that fire-soft darkness they lay half-entangled still, that as if dozingly at last she murmured, "Only Hugh does she— Have other women felt devoted to you like this too? . . ." having now in any case, all things considered, beyond doubt some sort of right to ask.

So, finally, he had to look at things as they coldly were. And were, whether Alexandra was still alive somewhere in a looted and burning city or not.

———————
I I
———————

Eighteen, nineteen hours now she was gone. Though back well past that, faint dawn again it must have been, the second day's rioting had woken him. And he thought worse than the first, huge mobs scattering out before police. And it had gone on, half the city in wild disorder now, out of control it seemed altogether. And in that mindless tumult Alexandra these long hours vanished no notion where.

And she'd quit him without so much as a kiss—turned on her elegant heels with that final "You *can* be a tiresome pet at times my sweet can't you!" cool English voice taut with displeasure, out his door and down to her car in his courtyard and off into the soft Tuscan morning, unwarned, to meet her husband's plane.

Then, perhaps an hour it had been, the great pleasant trusting chap's voice on the phone: "Hugh? Aubrey here. At the airport. Any clue where Alex might have got to? Was to've met me, she tell you? Nothing could have held her up, surely? Not to worry of course, nothing I hope like that. But she was to have *met* me! . . ." And then, toward noon, the questura had reported her burnt-out car.

—Yet here now was he, Hugh Tatnall, a year her lover, no more concerned you'd have thought in this agreeable bed than if she'd (say) merely gone out of town and nothing beyond an offhand infidelity were the point, a mere role in the usual masque, instead of that subtle body he knew by heart lying it might be battered and unidentified in some nighted emergency ward, or in a lightless alley or down an embankment even, still to be found. If indeed alive at all.

Except why on earth anything of the sort!—Alex, if anyone ever, serenely looked after herself. As to her car, for whatever reason why, simply she'd abandoned it.

Reason moreover might very well be, if some part of the rioting it was had stopped her, she'd amused herself by joining in—the English upper classes had been having fun in worthy demonstrations ever since Spain in '36.

Why in short should anything melodramatic have happened to her at all? That being the *off* chance.

And why assume she hadn't already turned up safe and sound hours ago anyhow!

—A letter from his London agent it had been began it: did he still now and then rent a friend that other half of his piano nobile? Because a friend of *his*, chap named Fonteviot, many years' friend in fact, known him since Oxford, been up at Merton with him, 'd rowed for the College, *charming* great man, and now it happened he wanted a pied-à-terre in Florence—was just it appeared adding factories near Prato and also at Empoli to the main complex of plants he owned in the Piedmont. Wife elegant Anglo-Irish; in fact very nearly a great beauty. Likelihood was they'd want the apartment for a good year minimum. "Ce sont de braves gens, Hugh—and the lovely Alexandra's an absolute Gainsborough for you." Or, he'd said to himself, a Van Dyck: sounded a bit that *Countess of Clanbrassil* sort of thing in the Frick. Though anyhow why not? So in due course she'd come from London to have a look.

And his connoisseur of an agent had been right: a beauty by god she was, Gainsborough or not. He'd been grinding pigment when she came; he was a mess; it amused them both. He showed her through "l'attraverso"; they strolled slowly, even dawdled, as she looked at everything, room by room, with little courteous cries and murmurs of pleasure—what a heaven of a palazzo he had, what a blessing it all was, what pictures what tapestries, what a great angel he was to be willing to rent it to her: the whole bland polished extravaganza of British upper-class rhetoric. They'd pleased each other at sight.

Later, Fonteviot too had seen and liked it. In due course they'd moved in. He had given a couple of dinners for them (though they knew people already). They saw a good deal of one another; he did a Gainsborough of her after all; Fonteviot gave him a Degas sketch of Mary Cassatt.

Then, one day, and this had been a day of sudden wild spring cloudbursts which, shopping, she'd got caught in— great splattering gouts of rain bursting on those stone streets, the gutters a rushing flood, whirlpools racing ankle-deep over the drowned cobbles, and he had spotted her poised in stylish dismay in her jeweler's doorway, trapped aghast in the utter crash and din of it. He had skidded his car in to the curb and flung open the door shouting to her, and she'd leaped from the doorway and with happy little yelps of laughter skittered in beside him. *What* a godsend he was, in pure relief her lilting English voice told him, these *damned* brutes of taxis that wouldn't stop for one! shaking raindrops over him from her hat, from her gloved fingers; and half the way home, as he wove through the deafening wet hiss of the traffic, she fumed at it all, for what nameless Florentine pigs they were, what a canagliaccia!

Though then in the courtyard of the palazzo they had to sit on in the car, waiting for the deluge to slacken, the rain now coming down in great ropes, beating on the flooded cobbles, so fierce it leaped up again knee-high almost, drumming on the car roof till they barely heard each other.

So, waiting, they'd agreeably gossiped; and presently he had told her how he'd just got a fresh-caught Loire salmon flown in, from Nantes, he was going to have it cold with that green mayonnaise of his Lucrezia's, so why wouldn't she and Aubrey come take lunch tomorrow? it being Sunday.

But *how* wonderfully kind of him, she'd cried formally, that lovely food that absolute jewel of his did for him; but she said—

With that same wine (he put in) which, last time they'd had dinner with him—

But now he was making her *totally* despairing, she wailed as in sheer good manners, that heavenly hock of his, but didn't he remember she'd said Aubrey was off tomorrow for Zurich again, early?—those squalid bankers of his adored the place, *oh* how it all put one out! and just when he was offering her this lovely lure of his, his Loire salmon.

Out of nowhere, no more than the word "lure" even it may have been, or the lingering caress of her lips shaping it—who knows why, ever?—suddenly he was so breathless with the sense of her, and so shaken at what he found he was about to say, that he did not see how he could say it without faltering. But she, though, surely (he managed to get out, holding his breath, for what if she knew as well as he that this was not what he was asking), at least *she*'d come, wouldn't she, Aubrey or not?

But he *knew* she never stayed when Aubrey took off, it was detestable and she was bored, she took off herself (she told him, great eyes all gentian-blue light suddenly deep in his), she simply got into her car—"Me ne vo e basta!" didn't they say? she'd seen *immense* parts of Italy. Though this time she'd go she thought see her brother, he'd just bought a villa on the Corniche beyond Cannes, she adored him, it was all arranged.

So he had taken a deep breath and said but couldn't she be at least tempted into leaving *after* lunch? Or good god he said (since what he was asking was not what he was asking) even next day?

So for a long moment she looked at him and anyone might have thought she was only thinking how surprising.

All however she then said was a faintly mocking "Si figuri!" and the rain having at last abruptly stopped they went in. At her door she said, "Aubrey's plane's at eleven," and he answered, "Come at three then?" and she slid her heavy key into the slotted brass of the escutcheon, let her eyes rest on him for one long cozening moment, and then, wordless, was gone.

He let himself in his own door as breathless again suddenly as some dazzled boy, for such beauty for oneself who can ever quite believe it? for as anybody could see, it had been decided.

Next day though it might have seemed an ambiguity of caprice they blandly lingered on in, over the splendors of his salmon, the cool cheeses, the crimson dunes of wild strawberries on their paillasses of bright leaves, the torrone molle they left untouched at the end, spinning out instead the slow enchantment of unspoken enticements and acquiescences on and on into the long murmuring afternoon, the approach of night as if hardly yet in their pulses, only this comedy of unavowal still to be played out to the last unneeded word—time itself in fact one unsurfeitable luxury the more to them, that final feast of each other who cared when it was to come. So they were long; it was delight.

Or as he had thought once, many hours gone—deep night then it was, though still for neither of them the night at an end or for discoveries near it even, his senses so drenched with her by then they hardly recorded what elegance of line the draftmanship of his tracing fingers told him her body was making love with such goddess-given luck (he'd said to himself) making love being with luck like this a pleasure not a conquest it can seem never to be over, never, even when one is in it it is not to be believed how it is, for what savoring of herself as of him she indulged him with, even the mockery of her "So unbridled, goodness!" a wantonness to lure him on.

Very late, too, and if they had parted his tall curtains and looked this might almost have been the first cool pallors of dawn, she had said, lightly adrift up over him, sated at last and amused, "Though how frightful, having to seduce one's men! M'ma always gave one to understand it was the other way about."

He was too dazed with her still to think of anything, even mindless, to say.

"Or did you fancy you were luring me to the lovely wickednesses of your bed with a *fish*?—goodness what middle-class guile!"

He made an effort against his stupor: she had upper-class reasons instead?

"Well may you uninnocently ask!" she murmured, and in their eclipsing darkness slithered like a lovely dolphin back down into his arms.

—And it was *this* enchantment, he now had to say to himself, *this* angel he might conceivably never see again, for who can ever even expect them until in pure wonder there they are. And now, it was possible, there no longer.

For a bad morning he and Fonteviot had had of it. She'd have gone, for they thought surely how else, out the Via della Scala, then by the Via delle Porte Nuove and so on straight to the airport. So each had worked from his own end, Fonteviot in toward the city, he outward to meet him, phoning hospitals and the questura first. No word of her at any of them; and soon Fonteviot phoned, frightened now: he'd drawn a blank too—taxi'd been stopped by a damned police block at his end of the Via della Scala, flat refused to let him through. So he'd turned back and covered the Via delle Porte Nuove and the Via Toselli and so forth back to the airport again. Not a sign of her car. Nor in the airport park either.

So they'd had to look along the Via della Scala on foot, each from his own end. But at the Via Santa Caterina intersection he himself had come near being turned back—police vans and a jeep stood end to end across and he was having no luck at all talking his way through when there was this muffled sudden uproar from the direction of the station off to the right, shouting, and all at once thick black smoke came up over those buildings in great rolling spirals, then they heard bursts of tear gas and the police started piling into their vans and shot away, sirens howling.

So in the confusion he'd bolted, and got through. He had made it nearly to the intersection of the Viale Rosselli before he saw Fonteviot lumbering along toward him, and no trace of her.

So then to search the cross-streets (for who knew?) they separated.

For also she might they saw have taken the Via Palazzuolo route instead, or, again, around Santa Maria Novella and past the station. So Fonteviot turned off toward the Arno along the Via Rucellai and he himself up the Via degli Orti.

At once though he saw he'd get nowhere. Around the station it was chaos. The mob had it seemed run but the whole piazza was choky with tear gas, and police were beating up a handful of stragglers trapped against a wrecked shop-front and dragging them off to the vans. Just in front of the station four bodies lay sprawled by an overturned kiosk; they looked trampled. In front of a hotel opposite, great licks of flame and black smoke were rolling up out of a burning tanker-trailer; the hotel's façade was scorched; glass had shattered from its windows, in the heat, and muntins were catching fire.

It was the questura reported her burnt-out car: been driven they said up onto a sidewalk in the Via degli Avelli. So she must have tried to bypass some block or other and gone round behind Santa Maria Novella toward the station. So during a silent lunch they took turns phoning hospitals.

Presently, though, the questura rang up again: now they had found the signora's handbag. Tossed aside, it appeared, against a wall of the church. The signora's driver's license was in it, yes, but if there had been valuables, these they regretted were gone. So Fonteviot had taken off for the hospitals: no unidentified admissions now meant nothing, emergency wards everywhere were traboccanti they said with casualties and more constantly being brought in, *many* more, as the rioting spread. Nothing therefore to do but make the rounds, hour after hour, until, somewhere, she might be brought in.

He himself hadn't even that to kill time with.

In a doomed way, then, presently, in the studio he took out his portfolio of sketches he'd done of her. That whole year's worth, and he went through them slowly, thinking as he looked at each drawing, and remembered the act of drawing it, of the day he'd done it, the circumstances of her pose, the light, what else too they'd done that day in particular; the stage of happy desire for each other their knowledge of each other by then had brought them to; almost he thought now and then as he looked at these images what *was* she then? on the day of this sketch or that, what had she felt as he worked? for now it had begun to occur to him that possibly he had never actually known. He came on a charcoal they'd had a row over. A sheer petulance: she'd been doing her face at her glass and he was sketching her with amusement and she had got very cross, he no longer remembered why, only the unpleasantness. Which had lasted a week nearly. He put the portfolio back in its drawer.

An elderly jest came into his mind of his rich old libertine of an uncle's, whose palazzo this once had been: "Popes have those endless sequences of lady saints. Humble laymen like you and me, my dear boy, must make do with an occasional pagan goddess." In his uncle's day the studio had been a ballroom.

It had its baroque balcony still. He stepped out, aimless, thinking of ways he had seen the light fall on the planes of her face. Over across, the French windows of the Fonteviots' balcony stood open too. Somewhere on inside a maid was singing as she cleaned, *Ahi che mi hai fatto, Amore*, and in abrupt desolation he saw in his memory that summer evening Alex and he had lain here, here on his old uncle's great rococo divan, stilled suddenly as lovers turned to marble, unbreathing, listening to Fonteviot come in across and wander nearer calling her name through those other rooms and out at last onto that balcony across, murmuring by then in bafflement and deep disquiet a no more than whispered *Alex? . . . Alex?* . . . for where could she conceivably be?—and this was what, for all he could tell, he himself had now lost too.

Early June that had been, afternoon he remembered faded already into the edges of night, and next day it was she and Fonteviot were to be off, at daybreak, for England; trunks long since packed and gone, maids sent on ahead; be away from him poor libidinous sweet till grouse season, she'd cooed at him; even beyond, even; goodness how often he'd have trompée'd her she expected by then! and kissed him sweetly laughing goodbye.

But for one last farewell sight of her still he'd gone across the landing later again anyhow, and in. The place was stripped, sheeted away for summer, furniture shrouded white, dim now already with coming night, the tall formal rooms a silence of unstirring air, hooded pictures lost in shadows—life could have been gone, nightfall and abbandono everywhere. She had heard his key clatter in the door, and come quickly from somewhere deep in the house; he had got no farther than the piccolo salotto. Though how could she have known the key was his?—for perhaps instead it was his footfall she had heard as he came looking for her through those rooms that were nighted now and echoing, floors shining dark-polished in the summer dusk. She was in white, or white in that now deep obscurity it seemed to him: hair twirled up into a high Italian knot, and she had stuck a peacock's feather through it; and what on earth did he want now? for she was writing letters.

So he had said, deprecative and half in jest, resigned, for in any case it was all too far past hope to risk asking for in English, in English in fact the phrase was so childish-sounding that for months it had been a minor ritual joke they made now and then about making love—he'd said in his best mock-sospirante voice Nemmeno he supposed *una* ultima volta di più? ... and what had the angel done but laugh and it was like a miracle, indulge him with the ritual's mocking reply, "*You* ever just *one* last time more? Ho!"—it was unbelievable what luck it was, and back across to his studio they'd sprinted (or by god as good as!) without another word.

But then soon they had heard Fonteviot. From the salotto it sounded he called her first, just come in, calling with bland assurance, where was she? though then coming nearer through those great hooded empty rooms in the now fading light, calling now in a sort of soft surprise, "Alex? Where've you got to? ... Alex!" But then soon with less confidence, indeed there was now an edge of panic in that pleasant voice, "Alex aren't you here? What's happened dammit? *Alex!*"—the big man hurrying now, tiptoe as if swift with dread, calling nearer and nearer her unanswering name, till there out on that balcony across finally he stood, emptily staring, knowing now she was not there, not anywhere, it was pointless, yet still whispering, in a mere rustle of breath, his baffled *Alex? ... Alex? ...* into the gathering night.

In an instant, at that first far-off sound of her name, she was up out of their embrace, breath caught, fiercely listening, at bay —pitched up half over him still on one Botticelli arm, hair tumbling, and in its dim tent what he could see of her eyes might have been a gaze of marble, unseeing, down into his own. They lay transfixed, wild. And as shapes he thought can in the dark silver of mirrors at night loom out of some menacing perspective of shadows and suddenly it seems they are upon you, so these lovers could each have been watching, in fearful vigilance, for that image the other's mirroring pupils might at any moment hold, the great bulky pleasant unsuspecting man blundering through those darkening rooms toward what they both knew would be his heart's dismay, handsome face even now chapfallen, the bafflement beyond human explanation. And, as he came, calling.

Till there on the balcony across then he'd stood, twenty foot away if that, the sound of her name no more than that dumfounded whisper.

Then that too died away on the nighted air; and suddenly with a soft fluttering throaty sound he'd never heard her make before—ferine, erotic, seigneurial, derisive, God knows what —down her head came in a lovely arc seeking his mouth, and her body slid back down onto his.

—Never *had* found out what explanation she'd offered Fonteviot afterwards. A scribbled note thrust next morning under his door said merely

Va bene here my sweet, have a pig of an Italian summer. But then *I* shall be back, remember!—trilling 'Ere I calm wiz a rose in my teece, anch'io!

signed with a lipstick kiss.

I   I   I

All of which now, in the shadowy fire-soft landscape of this bed, this lovely child might for all he knew have decided she had earned a supplanter's pitiless right to explore, even intrude upon, though this for the moment he could not tell, the hearth's ruined and dying crimsons now barely breathed into that dusk it was so deep, also she lay close, he could not see her eyes to tell; for in any case, as if in this new wild flooding of her senses beginning never to want not, or shyly learning, her soft young mouth had just kissed his throat now he seemed so lovely to her.

He thought damn all women, the things they are capable of saying! for when this one asked impossible questions what possible answer did she in heaven's name think he could make to her?

Ah, but then, he said to himself, but then they all do, wherever, this off-chance ritrovo or a civilized bedroom and long love, not seeing he supposed that we can only lie and they what but be made frightened we do. And it is from pure egotism, less to please than to make sure they please more; so go even as far as there *has* been what they seek to know and the truth (or whatever) is more heartless still.

Even bringing their hopeless questions up they suffer, he as good as said aloud: they know beforehand they will suffer and that if we love them we must lie.

And as this one, either, didn't see it should never have been asked, or that it is always impossible, indecent even, then the child was in for more sconcertamento than a first roll in the hay ought to involve any girl in as much an angel as this one. So he hoped she'd drift asleep, and then forget. And with luck why not? for he felt her soft breath in the hollow of his shoulder, soft as dreams.

But from her nightfall lawns of silence now she settled closer against him and this he supposed she did to seem to confide or the like rather than what he called explore, for as if meek she now said, "Or I guess you don't really though think I ought to ask, do you."

This being neither a question to put nor the way to have put it even if it were, it was perhaps apology, though in the rose-depths of darkness they now lay in she seemed to have opened her dreaming eyes and be looking at him, as for some reply, for he felt her long lashes brush his ear.

(Though however he might reply he did not see how she or any woman could believe him. Women they would not be if they did, and this was why what a folly such questions were, so he said nothing.)

Anyhow she went on, as if explaining, "Except Hugh I have you know seen you and Mrs. Fonteviot, well, *look* at each other. At parties I mean. I mean when I sort of thought you didn't think anyone was noticing. Twice," she said.

So damn all their intuitions too, he said to himself, they are fabulous, they are trained to see love everywhere so those eyes that it seems to us are like great jewels miss nothing anywhere, an unknown girl's eyelids cannot flutter a wordless *Soon* to her lover across some milling company to drive him wild with fatuous lust but they see it; or if he is near her it is not even the secret smile in the iris and for him alone that is secret from them—why, paint itself he thought cannot show what they see! and he said, "What worldly nonsense."

For a submissive moment therefore she was silent again.

—And his old libertine of an uncle's goddesses too, he thought, those elegant idle worldly girls, though to the small boy he had been they seemed old as his uncle (but who was then of course in fact as young as they)—his uncle had lived a lifetime being put through it like this, girl after girl at him as so to speak her turn for it came and often they must have wept with rage, he'd once himself in wide-eyed six-year-old bewilderment heard a molten young Roman beauty as good as raving at the man, screeching even. Absolutely primitive-wild, and he had thought, stunned, "Le donne have tantrums too? . . ."

Sheer opera; and now here was this one of his own.

—Who however appeared to have turned dreamy again for the moment instead. Even adoring, though it might have been this also was apology, for moving murmuring closer still she said softly it was so strange, she'd never imagined one would feel sort of "well, Italian-second-person-singular about you," she mumbled, mouth against his neck. "Mi *piaci!*—what a lovely thing to be able to say, *oh* it sounds so nice! Mi piaci piaci piaci piaci—and ti voglio bene too, don't I! oh it's so *convincing* in Italian!"

"Also safer," he said, and smiled.

But this she seemed not to understand, in fact only nuzzled

his collarbone and was silent so long, warm there against him in the fire-fluttered shadows, that he half-dozed.

Except then, and this too might have been in apology, this child went back to explaining: "But Hugh even before she introduced us I'd wondered *whether*. You don't have to remember I know but she'd taken me to that party at the contessa's, I'd only just arrived in Florence, I mean I didn't know anybody and of course not you then either, I didn't even know you lived here, goodness how surprised I was! Except naturally I knew who you were, after all I'd *studied* you hadn't I? I'd even wanted to do my course term-paper on you, only this professor was insane about the Chadds Ford school so he wouldn't let me, anyway you came in terribly late, even for Italy late, I was talking to that Curzio Saetti near the door, because I was thinking Mrs. Fonteviot looked very bored and was nearly ready to leave anyhow, and there you came in right *past* me! Though of course you didn't know I was, well, *me* yet, anyway I thought you were looking for your hostess, Mrs. Fonteviot had told me everyone here is terribly formal, even Americans. But then I thought *were* you looking, because you didn't seem even to glance round for the contessa, you went straight to Mrs. Fonteviot. Though I mean all I thought *then* was heavens that's *Hugh Tatnall the painter* and I was breathless, I thought but then she knows him! *my* Mrs. Fonteviot knows him! and I was just amazed—why, I'd only presented my godmother's letter to her the week before and now here you were! But then almost at once she came over to me and said did I mind if she ran me back to my pensione now? it was almost time for the party to begin breaking up anyway it was so late, so we left. But at the pensione when I turned round at the door to wave good night to her in the car, why, she'd turned on the dome-light and was doing her mouth in the rear-view mirror! So I was astonished, I thought is she going *back* to the party? Or *some*where, anyway not home! only then why hadn't she said so? and I thought how strange. Though there wasn't of course any reason for her to tell me what she was perhaps going to do. Because really there wasn't. But then I remembered all of a sudden that you'd just come in and said something to her, it took no time at all, and almost right off she'd come and said it was time to leave. So don't you see, Hugh? later I wondered, was all. But about Mrs. Fonteviot please I wasn't trying to pry, Hugh. But just to sort of tell you you didn't have to explain it," she finished.

Though then after a brooding moment, as he said nothing, she added in a gentle voice, "Then there was that one other time," as if she did not see how he could possibly need reminding.

When this one other time might have been, however, she did not go on to say, instead seemed to explain again:—

"All Hugh I meant was, I did wonder. Because you weren't you know *just* terribly nice to me once I'd met you, you paid attention to me as if really you were thinking about me—me as *me*. So naturally I did begin to think about you. I don't mean like, well, like *this*, really Hugh I didn't. Except I guess anybody always does a little don't they, even if only as hypothesis sort of, but I thought there you *were*, the way you are, famous and pratico del mondo and charming, goodness *any* woman would wonder who you—I mean *everybody* here it seems to be understood *all* the men have mistresses, don't they? Of course I'd read about cavalieri serventi during the Romantic Period, Lord Byron for instance and that Contessa Guiccioli. But that was *then*, centuries ago. Or two centuries nearly, anyway, and then there were all those bel mondo women Stendhal's autobiography tells about his affairs with when he was consul at Civitavecchia, though I didn't think it always sounded as if he'd actually *slept* with them very much. So Hugh I wondered. Because you certainly didn't seem to pay any special attention to any of Mrs. Fonteviot's Italian friends. Or any Italian women. Or do you think I shouldn't have noticed that either," she said humbly.

He was amused, and thought for a moment of telling her, and almost did, no no, bel mondo seduction-Italian it took an expatriate to be good at. Like an old uncle of his own, his mother's brother: been as good as irresistible to the wives of the local nobility. Delinquent English ladyships too, off and on: made for variety. But in principle'd lived off the country, what old campaigner didn't.

—But he could not upset this rueful child further still! she was lost as it was in sad uncertainties, one unintended seducer was bad enough good god without the debaucheries of an irrelevant uncle to be overcome about too!

But soberly, and in particular, was he heartless?—he could not let her go *on* seeking comparisons like this, what was there in mere innocence of the world, in simply being young, for her to upset herself over!

Also he was a little upset about it again himself.

So he lolled her gently up out of the curve of his shoulder and slid her to where in those dying shadows he could make out her fire-lit eyes, which now he thought looked at him so uncertain she might once more not be feeling sure of anything about him, even whether he wanted her to smile.

In mere kindness therefore he said look, wasn't it time she began to see that this was—for want of a sensible word—normal? this being how it did happen. Foreseen or not was he told her hardly the point: making love was always it seemed somehow new and unexpected, and who you made love with always this stranger, always new, this lovely phoenix. Which was why making love he said, stroking her, was an exploration he did not see how he or any man could ever come to an end of or want to—here was this Being in your bed, this secret presence, and what could you feel you'd ever want more on earth than to discover who she was, this charming stranger.

And added, to make it sound less ponderous, off-chance it could even be Aphrodite herself, he said amiably, thinking of his uncle, for why not? *had* been for Anchises!

So she looked at him with solemn eyes. Believing. Even it appeared memorizing. As how beautiful. As (in hopes any-way) the Mystery itself.

At any rate she came up gently onto an elbow over him, to gaze down at him now it almost seemed with the sweetness of trust, this grave brooding gaze. "Then really do people then?" she asked presently. "Because I never I guess thought of any-body's thinking about love that lovely way. But Hugh *men* don't though, do they, surely?"

Ah, well, no, he said, the information was most didn't, shift-ing his arm that had lain under her, up agreeably over and around, fingers tracing the elegances of that docile young back, downwards too, thumb modeling the plunge of waist into slender thigh. "No real notion what they're even doing," he told her in mild derision, in self-gratulation too in fact it sounded (though under the circumstances why not?). "Here's this lovely labyrinth of you to explore, good as *waiting* to be explored, mind you! and they don't even suspect it! Past be-lief," he told her great soft eyes. So the breathtaking (you'd have thought) question *who* this angel is, right there in their arms to be asked, they never he said think of asking—though for all they know about her she could be some total appari-tion, not three-dimensional reality by god at all. "Whereas the fact is, only *you* know it non è vero? and no more than part of the time at that," he ended, laughing at her, and taking her charming waist in both hands he woggled her tenderly.

This she paid no attention to, but gazed down at him there as if wildly absorbed, as at practically a revelation, eyes poring over his face.

So ecco, there was the reason, he concluded it, why the average man wasn't much competition—a truth however of so little conceivable interest to any girl, in bed with him or not, and here, with this one, so irrelevant, she did not even bother to hear it.

Saying instead, in a musing voice, "But then Hugh how

does anybody get over feeling shy if it's always still strange? Because partly, maybe, I feel shy because Hugh I just don't know enough about making love to *guess* what you think about me! I—feel so—I don't even know how to *say* it! I almost feel like the girl I roomed with sophomore year, she'd been frantically trying to decide to go to bed with some boy, because you may not know it but virginity can be very difficult *socially* at college if nothing else, but she couldn't make up her mind for months because Hugh it *is* everybody says so much a toss-up with just boys. But finally late one night she came back to the room looking sort of totally astounded and said, 'Well, I've finally *done* it!' in this bewildered voice, but then what she said about how it had been didn't make it sound as if she was at all certain she felt as impressed, for instance, as she thought she ought to, only she didn't even know whether this *was* how you felt. I don't mean she thought was this *all*, disappointed I mean or whatever, because she said it *was* really fantastic in a way, but she just seemed terribly baffled by not having any way of deciding whether what she felt was *standard*, sort of, was this what one *does* look for, aside from all the bliss-propaganda. It had seemed so unspecial she sounded practically *alarmed* Hugh about it! And the boy had been no help. Even whether anything had gone on in his head about her she couldn't imagine, he looked so stupid. *Nothing* might have happened between them! In a way she said she supposed it was in principle special, being this First Time, but about *him* she didn't seem to feel anything special at all, even trying to. Or trying to feel 'tender.' Or seventh-heavenish and swoony. She just didn't! Also what was silliest of all, she said, she didn't even begin to know whether she was, well, *you* know, 'any good'—or whether this boy was either, how *was* she to know! So she was practically out of her mind with exasperation at how little about making love she'd even found out—emotionally she didn't seem to have learned anything more about it afterwards than she'd known before. Which meant she therefore actually knew less! And she's the only girl I've ever talked to *really* about making love, Hugh. In depth that is. But now here about *you* nothing she said seems to make any sense at all, it just doesn't *apply*—or the way you described it either, so how can I help being confused? Especially when the way I seem to feel about you—well, I just *feel!*" she cried as if helpless. "I don't even think what other girls say makes much difference, I wouldn't have known what to expect any more than I did. Because I'd never have expected *this*," she said, collapsing tenderly on him again. "Are you just sort of specially charming, or what?"

So he said a mildly deprecating "Hoh!" to her; but he thought, at least she sounds deflected from Alex.

And decided to encourage the diversion. Other girls, he therefore said he agreed, probably were little help. Women, anyhow, he suspected, didn't discuss lovers with other women, except to boast, or to disparage—or find fault, like that roommate of hers. Or of course to swap hilarious indecencies of detail now and then. But a love affair that deeply pleased them was it seemed a secret sweetness, there was no delight so deep, why shouldn't they hug it to themselves? And afterwards often its memory too. It was lovers women were pleased with they "talked" to, not other women, if to anybody. Was she for instance going to tell her roommate about *this* night?

"When I've been *silly?*" she cried, shocked, whirling up over him on her elbow again, curls tumbling wild.

He said oh nonsense, she didn't actually any longer think she'd been "silly" dammit, why pretend, anyhow she knew quite well she could offhand dream up twenty plausible explanations for her roommate of *how* it had happened, what was woman's angelic imagination for?—it wasn't the circumstances, no, it was the lovemaking she and he had so entranced each other with.

"But Hugh I did everything in such a—in oh this schoolgirl helpless way!" she mourned.

He said was she past belief too? trying to tell herself she hadn't *felt* every lovely atom of her was in it as headlong as he!—how could she have more?

"Oh I know how I feel, I don't mean I've been too busy being dazed with you not to know that," she said soberly. "But I can't very well know, can I, whether this *is* the way anybody who's had all these very affectionate attentions of yours should feel, don't you see that? Or *do* girls ask about other girls?"

He supposed not particularly, he said, more or less lying.

"About how they—what happens."

She meant *she* wasn't asking?

"No but for instance Hugh I know this will sound silly but how does an Italian girl start calling a man she likes 'tu' instead of 'Lei' without sort of giving her feelings away to him, how does she keep it from being terribly abrupt-sounding? Because it doesn't often happen like, well, *this*, does it?" she mumbled, abashed. "But in English, with 'you' for everybody, it's simply not a problem that ever even occurred to me existed."

Why, Italian girls he didn't much know about, he told her (and this was a sensible lie). But the "problem" would, he expected, be more likely not language nuances but the cultural differences people grew up with. The bred-in assumptions wouldn't match, for instance the signals one learned about the other sex's Yes and No. Because anybody's behavior was helpless routine like the rest of the damn' populace's. Except of course painters', he added, and patted her, smiling.

These generalities she appeared however to see no point in. "Well, but what I meant," she said, going back, "was for instance the first time a girl sleeps with a man? Stays I mean the night, so there is this next day, and it *is* all strange, Hugh part of *me* isn't even sure it's still me, what happens to one's ordinary reflexes about even trivialities seems to be just wild! So what sort of thing does the girl for instance *say* when they wake up?"

—This nonsense *really* he said to himself it could not go on! at what point do they stop being apprentices and learn the full lustre of their beauty?

But he managed to say, teasing, good god had her professors got her to believing there was such a thing as answers? if a girl woke up in her lover's arms what *could* she say but whatever happened to come into her sleepy head? One flippant coquette he remembered had for example said to him just *Miss me?*

But the child did not seem to follow this either.

In fact, after a silence, "But about other girls," she said in an uncertain voice, "what sort of thing—I mean a *man* telling a girl about other girls?"

He was tired of it. Still, he conceded, had she been a blessing or hadn't she? so he said, gently or as good as, look, it was not a *question* of other girls, what were other girls? let her have the confidence her beauty should give her!

So for a long moment she gazed down at him, eyes dreaming and grave, as if pondering this; persuaded almost, spellbound.

"But Hugh aren't there ways?" she asked presently, stroking his temple with a fingertip. "I mean things I could do," she said apologetically, "except you're too darling to me about it to say."

He said "'Things'?" idly, fingers spanning that slim young waist again. "What things?"

"But which I don't *know*, Hugh!"

Ah but look, he said in pure indulgence, what on earth was there to "learn" or whatever verb it was she was fussing about? And anyhow basta with all these endearing *buts* of hers, wouldn't she in God's besought name *trust* him for once when what he told her was absolute truth? which was that she couldn't have *been* more Woman-a-paradigm-of-herself?— rolling her down beside him again where she was more convenient.

"You mean you're tired of all my amateur questions!"

"Outraged," he said, and pulling the child to him he kissed her enchanted eyes.

At which, mumbling "Oh Hugh . . . " she slid her arms as if in obedience around his libertine neck.

So, like any man of sense who'd had something as delicious as this practically god-given him, he saw, resigned, that clearly it would be considered a nonsense, after this gentlemanly interval, not to begin to think about having it again.

I V

Room cooling, it might have been, woke him.

Stuporous, in unknown black whelm of night no notion where; foundering; lost. And, next instant, mind a maelstrom: for this *who* was ——— ?

Then remembered. Who and where both.

And so gently it seemed she slept as if fondled there still, all blood-warm sweet against him, face tenderly smothering in his neck, softest breath riffling his hair.

Warm because warm he'd kept her.

Except at once this woke him further, for, to recapitulate, simply had that whole fire gone out?

So saw he had to ease an arm out from under, gingerly, to tilt half up, to see.

—Sunk to *ash* . . .

Stared at it in affront, blank, propped on an elbow in total darkness, mind saying *blast*.

—Though, then, blast or not, what was there for it but see to it? so, warily, had to try inching his legs from among hers, such pitch-black night it all was he could not even see how. But it did not appear she stirred. So, with extreme caution, touch-and-go still, he did work finally around to rolling slowly clear. But that eiderdown to cover her in his place, he could no more find feeling about in that blackness for than see.

Or find a dressing-gown they'd let fall either—till it was when he had slid stealthily out of the bed at last and fumbled his way along its swags and hangings he tripped into the things in a heap on the floor at the foot.

So he groped round to the other side with the eiderdown and spread it over his sleeping blessing, or as well over as in that blind dark he could guess at. Then back and picked up a vestaglia. Which he wrapped himself in, shivering.

But when he knelt and blew on the fire it was too far gone.

—Well, but surely a ritrovo as elegant as this one he decided would be run for all departments of benessere in general wouldn't it? this being Italy. For had no other secret lovers woken in this room to dying embers, or so sad a symbolism not been foreseen, to be provided against? and sure enough, when he felt about in the great brass hearth-box there was charcoal and those little drum-shaped bundles of neatly split faggots, even a sheaf of paper spills.

So, shortly, fire at least kindling again, he sat back on his heels staring into it, yawning.

It was slow. Charcoal was slow, catching.

So he dropped another handful of faggots on, loose. And this worked: the stuff caught in a burst—blazed up in so white a sudden dazzle the room's great cube of darkness was as if struck back, simply it fell apart into shards toppling every which way, it could have been huge shadows leaping frantic into corners. So, soon enough then, he could begin putting coals on, this first lump or two.

Sat watching it begin to glow, mind a pleasant blank.

Was warm again. No ambitions; just was warm. With those coals now slowly aglow. And himself warm. And three-dimensional: sensibility coming agreeably operative. *Himself* again.

—And aware that he could not, then, any longer, not phone.

If even for nothing more than find out whether.

To, at least, perhaps know . . .

—Nor could he lightly go on telling himself, either, hour after unexamined hour, that there would in any case be no one there to answer if phone he did, Fonteviot out plodding on and on through black streets and echoing squares, frantic by now, haggard, if by now he had not found her, or else at her bedside if he had, in a hospital somewhere or emergency ward, phoning pointless either way.

For now it had to be faced. Whatever, faced. He got to his feet and turned uneasily to the room.

Whose vaults of darkness were now filling he saw with the hearth's reanimated crimsons again, corners emerging, murmurous with soft dusk; and as if from aisles of twilight the bed loomed out now before him palely luminous, night gone from its tall canopies, through which the coals' fluttering images were cast so faint in under that where the girl lay he could not make out for sure, thickets of shadow were so dense, only the folds of the bed's hangings fell fire-dyed, damasks and wavering vermilions, and in the brocade of its swags glints of dull gold.

For a moment he was at a loss where they could have put the phone.

Though then her table de chevet he saw was where, and he thought *blast*, for suppose she woke.

But keeping his voice down why should she? Since anyhow phone he had to: could no longer not. So across he went, careful tiptoe.

Phone had call-buttons. He had to bend down, close over, to make out the etichette. *Direzione Maggiordomo Staffiere Cameriera Bar*: all Italy leaping to serve, to caress. He buzzed the staffiere and waited, staring at nothing.

"Pronto, signore!"

He said to the man, low, muffling the phone, ring this number he was giving him, would he kindly.

And, waiting, seeing in his mind that other table de chevet where now by her bed he heard her phone ring and ring, unanswered, he also became aware that what he was dully staring at, blank-blind before his face, was the Hermitage. He lifted it up near his eyes, squinting at it. A quarter full it looked still.

But barely cool. Moving with care, he stretched slowly off with it to the wine-bucket, phone-cord snaking after, and soundlessly eased the bottle back in. Out of anyhow the way.

Ice left or not.

"Non risponde, signore."

He muttered well dammit to keep trying.

Though turning now to look he decided the girl would not perhaps wake after all. For in those clustering shadows she lay it seemed almost as he had left her, unstirring, lapped in sleep, under the eiderdown he had spread over her (askew, he now saw), sweet young head half-smothering still in the pillow where he had lain, lashes as if dreamless on her cheek, though the hearth's burgeoning roses were too faint through those heavy hangings for him to be sure. And waiting there he stood gazing, simpleminded, savoring how it had been, the remembered pleasure of her—and this in a kind of wonder, even, for always how is it one has never, beforehand, quite seen the beauty, the amazement, of detail they can be; and suddenly *Alex* he heard his mind say to him, so that for a moment he was dazed with the uncertainty, totally lost, it could have been either of them lying asleep there, it seemed he had no way of telling which, the sweetness drowning his senses an enigma of memory forever; and he thought, with accusation, *I am unteachable*.

"Sempre nessuno, signore. Ma se ci vuol che—"

No he said never mind: non importava, and turned away. Though then good god he thought what was this heartless *non importa* when the night had still to go on! *on* and on and with nothing even to do. Or keep still, even, poking empty-minded at the fire.

He went to the window, and looked out, aimless, into the dark cortile.

Night outside was he saw no longer that immense cumber of shadows. For a moment, surprised, he thought faint glow it must be from some burning quarter of the city beyond was being shed down, reflected, from lowering cloud-mass. But it came and went, intermittent gulps of oily light, from it seemed off to his left. He leaned close to the panes to see, and it was an abandoned car, burnt out it looked but still burning sluggishly, gouts of dirty flame now and then; and in that light he saw what he had taken in the blackness earlier for some sort of small private square, or perhaps courtyard, now opened he saw at that far end onto a tangle of narrow streets, and these led off God knew where, into fathoms of darkness beyond.

A thin rain had been falling. The smoldering car as he looked flared up as if in a puff of wind, thousands of points of gold light burst up and fled scattering out over the wet black cobbles below him, so that for an instant he made out the whole piazzetta plain, end to end. Arcaded façade ran he saw the whole length over across, the arches rounded and their soffits picked out with eccentric abbellimenti of some sort in the stone, ball-flowers perhaps or crockets; and the severe march of long Roman bricks was broken, between the formal courses of the windows, by fylfots and enameled medallions alternating. Under the central cornice a baroque cramp-iron carried what looked like a date, or a scrolled initial. Architecturally it could be anything.

And a bare twenty foot out, below, was the fountain whose overflow splashing he had heard. Now he saw it was a Roman patera sort of thing: simply, water welled up through this low stem into the flat circle of its cup, to spill, thin slopping sheets of it, out over and down into the round stone basin its foot

stood in. At its imagined corners some later taste had set four
battered coehorns on the cobbles, linked by chains.

Then that abrupt flare of smoky light guttered and went
out, snuffed. It was black again.

And silent; or if sound came from the rumorous city beyond, of somewhere mobs still, it would have been like surf far
off among dunes in darkness, or like when in a cove at night
long seas roll in to burst thundering and thudding under the
rotting timbers of a jetty long years disused, and if the tide is
making it is a sound he thought as of an omen among ruins.

He let the long folds of the curtain swing closed.

—But turning away, to the fire-soft dusk of the room again,
now he could not think what there might be merely to do,
night it seemed was without end everywhere. He was mindless
with disquiet. For ring Fonteviot so soon again he could not,
in reason: no time had gone by. Or not enough, though in the
deeper shadows there by the window he found he could not
make out the face of his watch, to see.

But going toward the fire for light, he thought, with a kind of
sardonic dismay, was he God help him merely *bored?* . . .
For eccolo, here he was at a ritrovo with as sweet, as ac-
quiescent, a delizia as the Bona Dea and Iddio combined had
ever indulged him with, and in *this* situation he felt at a loose
end good god?—grumbling and put upon? . . .

—But all the same, night in fact lay before him for long
hours still. And whatever the time was (presently he saw),
was he to sit on and on in the dark doing undistractedly nothing whatever?—since going back to bed was he supposed not
possible, the child would be woken, and if then sadly shamed
again it would have been unkind.

So in his mind he tossed, fuming.

Having been exasperated further by discovering he could
not make out the hands of his watch at the hearth either, the
coals glowed too dim.

—Which on top of by heaven boredom was too *much!* if he

had hours of it still to face he'd at least find out how many!—
though then round the hooded bed he still stepped softly, wary
eye on that sleeping pleasure of his this time too.

Though, then, waiting phone in hand, he thought sardonically again what matter—was he any the less clear about this
probably misguided episode than if she were awake and prat-
tling? For what operators they are, he said to himself, even
novices they are capable of every disingenuousness. This one,
and after the happiest complicity, mind you—*three* complicities—Iddio Himself could not keep this one from arraign-
ing him for "seduction" if she decided to, lovely eyes wells of
betrayal and tears. When all he had done was humanely save
her, perhaps, from a fate as dejecting as her preposterous
roommate's—deflowered by an undergraduate, dear god what
a thing for any girl to have nerved herself up to! Whereas *he*
had helped her bypass disillusionment altogether, an absolute
beneficenza d'Iddio. Or of the Bona Dea's, it being of course
unknown Which happened to have the duty that evening.

Except that it was alas not he supposed clear to him what he
thought about this or perhaps any love. If only because what
girl is it one sees as she is, or even to herself is? so alike they
can seem. Alex too, even, he said to himself in depression:
each charming body as if beckoning up from the infidelities of
memory those ghosts of others'—so that again *unteachable* he
found himself saying in his mind, uselessly, or it may be he
muttered it half aloud, to whatever drifting presences glared in
rage at him from the shadows, torva tuentes like Vergil's
Dido; though in gloomy fact, he thought, it is all out of our
hands and is also hopeless, we lie to them out of decency, as
said. And often, likely as not, they lie to us from that strange
tenderness in return.

"Pronto, signore!"

He said, low, "Che ora è?"

"Signore? Quasi le tre, signore. Si fa tardi!"

—Fellow being *insolent?*

But no: no insolence in the tone. Not trained properly, was all, place being what it was. "Grazie," he said, and set the phone back on its stand.

—Two in the morning *then* it had been, not three, Alex had left him, merciless with anger.

And this, after a special lussuria of love long into the small hours—past surfeit they had even spun it on, for with Fonteviot returning who knew when such freedom could be counted on again: it was ritual. But then, and this she had never done on such an occasion before, she had taken him aback saying she must go—had he forgot she was to meet Aubrey's plane? And *early?* goodness! so go she must, too desolating, poor great lecherous sweet, but surely he could see? So they had gently wrangled.

Except that then, and from mere carelessness he said to himself it can happen in love—one wheedling word too many; the deftness of a caress misconstrued—abruptly it had turned out they were quarreling. For most *certainly* she would not stay! Had he no more sensibilità than a, than some lout of a, what was the word for a stableboy?—che uno stalliere, then! She did *not* propose to set out from *his* bed to meet Aubrey—in fact what an *utterly* squalid idea! And LET GO of her!

To which, in his folly, and he might have been some petulant mere boy, he'd very nearly replied what sudden onset of wifeliness made her fuss about which bed she started being faithful again from?—but, said or not, she had read it in his face; and though at the last he had appeased her enough to say she'd come have breakfast with him before she set out for the airport, she had left cold with displeasure still.

And gloomily now he had to say to himself God help him why not?—he'd as good as made a year's easy ambiguities explicit, insisting. Which bed, simply it mattered—if only for maskings and unmaskings of cool images in her pier glass, for unhurried complacencies, between sets of feelings and customs, and these for all he knew of her a bal travesti too. For what could he say she had ever been to his senses but a beck-oning masque from some *Assemblée dans un Parc*, smiling and heartless, some sweet Watteau marauder?—it having begun to be clear to him that he had not asked himself who, enchantment aside, this charming being had perhaps become.

Even that cold tantrum of Alex's it must be he had not known enough of her to understand. For it had hardly crossed his mind that she might not, by breakfast, be over it.

—In the curtained night of the bed the child mumbled something, and stirred, whimpering. He stopped dead, numb.

For, abruptly, so little about her he felt he knew either, that if now by bad luck he had woken her, bolt upright out of her pillows she could spring in the intake of a breath, eyes flying open at him wild, lips parted to shriek, at what deep terror he could never know; and then, as swiftly, all coming back to her—in a rush, everything—she might for all he knew feel oh what must he think of such frightenedness, and bunch down into the bed they had tumbled again, sheepish, overcome.

And if then in reassurance he went over to her she would humbly make room for him to sit on the edge there, slim body diffidently reassembling its symmetries of light and line, as if in apology drawing aside and away.

—But then, ah, well, his memory said, they can come awake mood anything.

They are an unknown, he said to himself, resigned; un-knowns, the lot of them; and what was he to make of this new one either?—for whether he was to regard himself as having (carelessly or not) acquired her, he did not see how it was possible to decide.

But for the moment it turned out she did not wake; so presently it was safe to step softly away, to the fire.

Which as he saw could do with more coal, he knelt and one by one took more lumps from the scuttle and put them on.

—The third morning this would soon be the chaos in the streets had gone on. Gunfire, that first one, he had thought it was woke him, and this had been very early—no more, it might have been, than first light, which fell, a pale bar, through some slot in the heavy folds of his bedroom curtains, this ingot of cool white gold. Or perhaps it had been tear-gas bursts, for when he heard it a second time it had those flat slaps of sound.

Though what matter which. He had dozed.

But then, sluggish, barely drifted up into waking again, with a pang he had begun to remember that ah, no farther off than tomorrow, now, Fonteviot was due; would be back, coming between, reclaiming, dispossessing; would *be* there, and his lovely Alexandra—though how he thought of her, sensual with sleep as he still was, was of the savors of that sleekness nightlong elegant and entwined, and at these splendors of remembered lust he had groaned longingly aloud.

Upon which, instantly, in his mind another English voice breathed to him, lazy with making love, though this had been in a bed in London, years gone, hardly the war over, *Tell me about your sweet lovely American girls, do they do all sorts of wicked wonderful things for you?* . . . light fingers stroking his belly, dream-crossed greedy body tangled with him still—except that then the sheer libertine faithlessness of all this had so amused him that he opened his eyes snickering.

So he yawned, happily, stretching.

And lay thinking about schedulings ahead, for tonight yes, but then Fonteviot back. Though he saw what was to happen was not clear. So then he had lain there, idly drowsing.

But at length had got up out of his bed and was shrugging into the sleeves of his dressing-gown, yawning still, when from what sounded some distance he heard shouting, from over across the Giardini it seemed to come, so he slung back the curtains from the French window and stepped through, to see, onto the little oriel of a balcony.

Up into the pale cool ivory of dawn—and it was beyond the gardens, on past the Strologaio corner too, where cold mist still coiled, or clung in wisps to walls, muffling them soft in wreaths of drifting white—up into the still air black smoke stood straight as a pillar just at the vicolo, and now he heard it had not been shouts, or articulate even, but a sort of toneless baying of sound, it could have been the sad bellowing of deaf-mutes.

And then this sudden flap of orange flame cut part of the mist through and he saw a camion afire, it was overturned across the vicolo, half-blocking the way into it; and just then this huge scattering mob, hundreds, had come pouring wildly out and around the other corner and in behind the Strologaio, and with a heavy clattering roar a police helicopter shot down past from nowhere over his head and scudded off low over the gardens as if in pursuit.

And police, he now made out too, had caught up with some of the last clusters of the running mob at the far edge over across, and were clubbing them.

He had said, "Well, be damned," a good deal surprised. But by then he was chilled.

Had gone back in and run a bath.

And when, presently, dressed, he had stepped out to look again, it had all seemed over. The camion, burnt out, they had pushed up out of the way onto a traffic divider. The uproar of the early Vespas was on.

Ominous who'd possibly have thought it! Riots are a European routine. They are politics; since votes are not.

He had even joked about it to Lucrezia as she served him breakfast: what had been that porco of a row that woke him —her Rivoluzione this time at long last?

She'd dismissed it with Marxist jeers: "Da dilettanti, signore! Da studenti!"

And "Tanto più fa paura!" he had tossed it off with, and gone on with orders for the day. He was lunching out. Expected no one for drinks. The signora inglese was coming to dinner. Start with an insalata alla Nizza, or some such, then he thought a rabbit, with that pine-nut and raisin marinade; and see if that fruttaiolo of hers had any wild strawberries yet. . . . *Now*, the light-mindedness of it left him stunned.

—And what that morning had she said and whirled on her stylish heels and gone out his door without a backward glance?—the cool displeasure he could remember, but the words she had flung at him, no. Yet why? When from deep tunnels of the past voices drift up like echoings in dreams, as if from those ancient catacombs and lost corridors of the self the waking self has never groped its way down to, they are so unknown. Yet so clear are they, almost it can seem those girls live on there, not memories but beings, and they speak.

—He could not stand it. He crossed to the phone and buzzed the staffiere one time more.

And as that far-off ringing began again, unanswered still, again he saw in his mind the tall cool room that for this whole year now the faint scent of her presence had made her own, and the scrolled and gilded pier glass that a thousand times must have held her image in its blackening depths; and from *it*, he thought despondently, her eyes would have looked out at her open and undissembling, as at no lover ever, but unguarded, primeval, solitary, all-knowing, and serene. But as for who the being is that looks out at us from the eyes even of our longest love or oldest friend, he said to himself it was as if there were the shimmer of a summer veil between.

—Then against all hope, so that believe it almost he could not, he heard, answering, Fonteviot's voice, ragged and fretful with it seemed fatigue: "Yes? Pronto—cosa c'è—chi parla?" but then, when he had said who, in a sort of headlong cry, "Hugh, *Hugh* where've you been! not still out *looking*, man, surely? Why in heaven's name haven't you rung in now and then—*hours* ago I ran Alex down! They've turned that old hospice into emergency and there the blessed woman was, fuming—couldn't make even the damn' sisters get word to me: language absolutely livid, *wonderful* spirits! She's a *bit*

knocked about, Hugh, broken collarbone and rather a nasty
scrape all down that side—got tumbled down one of those
flights of stone stairs by the river, running from the police. But
in *miracle* form, spitting fury at nobody's phoning me where
she was. Sent you her *love*. Where *are* you, by the way?"

He let the phone crackle on: now it made no difference.
Not only perfectly safe, Fonteviot was saying, but they'd bring
her home in the morning straight off. Was sleeping now, poor
sweet creature: he'd taken pills with him, in case, and given
her one. But Christ what a tamasha! Couldn't either of them
remember for the life of them when she'd had a tetanus
booster last. Thank God it was over. He felt *drained*. As, he
feared, must Hugh poor old chap too—he *was* most frightfully
sorry for the sheer bloody-mindedness they'd repaid all his
kindnesses to them by involving him in—these *Neapolitan*
unbridled Tuscans! But tomorrow, though, he *would* look in
on her wouldn't he? She'd want to thank him—been so quite
marvelously devoted and kind! So then see him tomorrow
then? Then good night, *must* try and get what there was left of
a night's sleep, he finished it, in a voice of now total exhaus-
tion, and rang off.

—Though it was of course tomorrow now.

In fact today; "quasi le tre" long past. In mere hours he
would see her.

As his mind did now—sitting up smiling he hoped at him
from her heaped pillows, eyes his again, a light hand out happily toward him across the sun-moted morning of her room for
him to lift to his lips, scattering her stylized English extrava-
gances of blandishment and apology into the glowing gold of
the air about him as he came, little courteous murmurs min-
gled it might be in, of penitence for what an *endless* night of
his it must, poor sweet, have been. . . . He would even be
thanked, the sudden sardonic gaiety of his relief said to him,
for this nightlong devotion, and no way to forestall the equi-

voco. He set the phone gently back on its stand and turned toward the bed.

Where it would be tomorrow-today sooner. And nothing for that either but wait.

—Except ah, he was tired of it. Wake, sooner or later, she had to. So hardly mattered by now if she did: be deep dawn before long in any case. He sat down on the corner of the bed where he'd sat before, and settled back against the tester-post, among the dark folds of the hangings, yawning.

In his mind, drowsily, he saw the first scene, how it might go. She lay mid-bed there; turned away; he would not see her eyes open. Drift perhaps then closed again, back into the last moments of oblivion: hardly conscious of seeing, of having taken in, the pillow her dreaming head lay lost in still. But then, again she would wake. She would make a little sniffling sound or two; would swallow a yawn; and then in faint surprise she would find herself looking at the unexplained curtains of this unknown bed, and her gaze would stray up, astonished now, to the tester-rails above. Then she would remember, and turn and see him; and, he hoped, would smile.

He would deal with it as it came.

With whatever matter-of-fact decencies of affection it turned out for the moment were called for.

—But for the tomorrows beyond? The structure of another scene to come rose in his mind like a tiny model of a set for a play, and this could well be no farther off than the real tomorrow. Alex would be abed still, recovering. But recovered enough for a levee. Friends would have been dropping in. With flowers, with fruit, with the jeweled rhetoric of bel mondo commiseration, with circolo scandal.

And in the particular scene his mind now saw, Rosemary would have brought flowers, and a book perhaps; and Alexandra would have patted the bed at her side and made her sit there; they would be amiably gossiping. He would have crossed the piccolo salotto, and the gilt and ivory of the anti-camera, and have halted in the white panel of the doorway, with a phrase of greeting. And as for that instant of pause he stood there, beginning to smile, those lustrous heads would turn to him as one, rosy tongues stopped in midsentence; and for a moment of absolute stillness, side by side, their eyes in wide unguarded welcome would be in his. . . .

—But first, as said, there was today. And this one.

He settled his head against the post's vased turnings and closed his eyes. He wondered, when she woke, what she would say.

PAYS
DE
CONNAISSANCE

I remember I thought, kneeling there in the blaze of that summer morning, how hot and still, how heavenly, it all might
have seemed to me instead, the towering château walls and the
neglected gardens in the enormous light, and the low-lying
green headland shimmering off à perte de vue to the immense
shining circle of the sea beyond, the whole world a brilliance
of enamel, turquoise and azure and gold, oh everywhere the
high summer I love and the sun like warm slow bombs, and
Hugh lounging there long-limbed and easy on the stone stair,
and looking at me; but of course by then none of all that was
how I could any longer see it, too much awful had happened, I
remember wondering how long it had been since either of us
had spoken even a word, and when at last he did, looking
straight at me with almost no expression at all, he just said,
"Why did you come with me?" like that.

I thought oh heaven as if I *knew*, and I said, "But Hugh
darling I love you, even after all this time I love you, I never
stopped," with my soft look at him under my eyelids to make
sure he believed me.

I did I remember wonder a little what that look of his was,
did he think I was heartless? as if that mattered!—though
mostly I was wondering whether now all this would perhaps
have spoiled things, making love: he might decide he saw it all
in my eyes like a tiny scene carved in a cameo, minute but
terribly clear—that empty Breton headland sloping up through
its meadows to the glitter of the ruined gardens and the sun
hot on the cobbles of the courtyard, the château walls over me

splintering light, and even under the great beeches in the parc around, sun splattering down through the foliage here and there like beads and coins of gold.

And when all this was just total mistake and tiresome!— and not the domaine Hugh had come to look over at all. But then, one winding fern-fringed ancient Basse Bretagne lane like every other till finally we were lost, and we saw this long avenue of huge old tilleuls leading back in from the voie to it seemed a wooded parc behind one of those rough-stone walls they all have, with wrought-iron gates standing open for once and an elegant little Renaissance lodge just inside, and, beyond, the avenue disappeared into the green gloom of the beechwood and I said to Hugh why on earth not drive in and simply *ask* directions. Of course he said, ". . . Just blandly intrude?" in his not-approving voice, so I had to say, "What a stuffy-Philadelphia darling you can be, goodness!" to get him to, only then there was no concierge at the lodge to ask.

So he said all right *all right* goddammit, though he sounded amused, and we drove on in, till after a minute I began to see glints of sunlight on masonry ahead through the green aisles of the wood, and suddenly out we came into the dazzle of a forecourt, under this great sun-flooded façade of rose-gray stone, up and up, balconies and balustrades and finialed cornices and an armorial escutcheon, prancing heraldic beasts and all, carved in the stone over the entablature of the portal, goodness what a place, and we rolled across the cobbles and pulled up beside four men in gunning jackets who'd just got out of a big black Citroën and turned to watch us drive up to them, and I remember saying to Hugh hunting in *summer?* except by the time I saw it was mitraillettes not shotguns in their hands they'd surrounded our car and it was too late.

One of them called out, "Va chercher le patron!" to a man in a blue houseman's apron who had just come round the far corner of the château, and then they just stood there looking at us empty-eyed—totally silent, and even when Hugh said,

"What the devil d'you think you're doing!" they just went on bleakly staring, and not a word.

I was thinking but Hugh speaks perfectly good French, why's he behaving as if he doesn't? when this tall man in riding breeches came hurrying out of the château with the blue-apron man, and the minute he saw the men around us he called out, "Mais non non non *non!*" and ran across the balustraded terrasse and down the half-dozen broad stairs down to the cobbles and over to where we all were, and I thought heavens what a beautiful man, bel homme doesn't begin to say it, he's breathtaking, but I supposed he was the "patron," anyway now he'd call these idiots thank God off, so we could go, how was *I* to know he couldn't.

But there at first he was so perfectly charming—and in English english, in the wilds of Outer Brittany of all places!—so perfectly distressed-sounding too about "this desolating over-reaction of his friends'" that really I don't see how I could have suspected, I don't think Hugh did either, then. Because we knew there *had* been this second or third attentat on General de Gaulle, and *Le Figaro* said it was believed the gunmen hid out in Brittany somewhere this time afterwards too, so when he stood there tall and elegant by the car, the sun on his fair hair and so exactly noonish overhead it threw the shadows of his eyelashes on his cheeks as he looked at me, goodness how blue his eyes were, I mean why *shouldn't* we have believed this wasn't a part of the general battue he said it was, "manhunt" didn't we call it in English? on battait la campagne all over the département, this back-country sous-préfecture in particular, and his friends had simply been over-zealous, but now *would* we have the gentillesse to let him try he hoped to make up for this lamentable malentendu by staying to luncheon with him? delayed as they had hélas by now made us, miles he feared from anywhere we could eat decently in any case? . . . so before Hugh could say no I started the process of saying yes we would by saying it was sweet of him but of course we couldn't. So of course he charmingly insisted —and if Hugh looked sardonic I didn't *care*. So in due course we introduced ourselves, he said he was Alain de Moëtland and Hugh said our name was Tatnall before I could stop him, and we went in; and it wasn't really till after lunch that we began to discover they wouldn't have let us leave anyway.

And then, not two days later, and oh so *sudden*, to have such savagery to remember . . .

—So I was still sort of in shock, kneeling there that lovely morning, though why I told Hugh I'd come with him was true enough if you felt romantic, because in a *way* I'd certainly wanted him practically from— Was it the winter I was nine? yes because Georgiana was nearly sixteen, he was taking her to a Penn Charter dance and Mummy'd asked him for the weekend, he was our cousin anyway. Of course I'd *seen* him before. Lots of times, I expect, but never the way *that* time he was, goodness!—he was like some fierce corsair the way he was after Georgie, he looked as if he could lunge at her right there in the drawing room and carry her off, and *she* I could see was absolutely in pieces about him inside—well, *ridiculous*, but it was an epiphany, my first-ever sense of Man after Woman, and *understanding* it! Of course part of me was sexy-wild, out of my mind over what was going to happen, but also I felt cold and brilliant all over, for now I *knew*, I can even remember the exact words I thought it in: *So this is how men are, wonderful and dangerous*, and I wanted to own him though I wasn't certain what for exactly, technically. Ho, but that night I found that half out too, I'd woken and gone to the loo and was just about to patter back along the dark third-floor hall when I saw him, he was tiptoeing, and I was *very* astonished, but just as I was about to ask him what he was doing he opened the door to Georgie's room, I remember particularly he didn't even stealthily knock, and he went *in!* Well, my heart was in ruins, I stood there simply out of my mind I've no idea how long, *oh* how I hated her, I seethed with it, I rushed back to my room and tried to listen to them through the wall, jabbering *D'you suppose he's kissing her?* to myself in rage and misery, and *Suppose she's* LETTING *him!* I plotted horrible revenges half the rest of the night, and at breakfast I sat glaring across the table at them till she got so upset and wild she tried to make Mummy send me away from the table. And later I stole a letter of hers to him, from the hall table, I loathed her so. But then I found all it said was "Each night I imagine our meeting. Shall it be where our lovely First was? Already I know what I'll wear, and how the sky will look, and you." So I didn't even bother to tear it up, goodness.

—Then on the passenger list there his name was. And I thought of all those times and times again I had seen him since, at dances and horse shows and family tennis and at weddings, he was an usher at both of mine, and how each time I would find myself being taken with him all over again, and I thought maybe this is the time nothing will stand in the way? and I sent the cabin steward round with a note to him. And in hardly any time at all there he stood in my doorway laughing and calling out, "Good god, angel, *you!*" and he was as lovely dangerous-looking as ever and I said, "Don't you ever knock?" wondering how I was going to keep my fingers off him long enough for ordinary good manners. But of course I did: it wasn't till the next day, he saw me back to my cabin after lunch and I couldn't resist saying, "Are you being charming, or just seducing me?" and it was lovely even the first time.

And that whole way across to Cherbourg, just lovely—I *never* thought I could spend so much that-sort-of time with a man, partly I suppose wild helpless girlish béguin I was working off years of, heavens some of my behavior! but oh a man sort of your whole body can feel knows what it is you do and how you feel inside doing it—by the night before we landed alarm bells were going off all through me, head and every-where, je m'en passais la fantaisie, yes, but what if I wasn't going to *recover* from this just anyhow! but then at dinner he

said look, whether I'd been describing us to myself as an affectionate experiment in symbiosis or just an extended roll in the
hay he was too out of his mind over me to care, but for *him*
there hadn't been anywhere near enough, there might never
be, the way he felt, he *adored* me and why didn't I come help
him try to find some for-sale manoir he'd told me he was
thinking of looking for, in Brittany, to buy for summers,
wasn't my French more than good enough to make American
fusses at the stingy inconveniences of their fruits-de-mer vacation hotels? and I thought of a phrase I'd read somewhere that
took care of the first part of his question too, and I said, "Ça
me ferait l'air de quoi, que de pester contre l'amour?" and at
Cherbourg his çar was the third up out of the hold, an *omen*
he said, so we'd have lunch at L'Avaugour at Dinan.

But we ran into the assassination alert even before we'd got
out of Normandy, on the straightaway after Avranches there
must have been half a mile of cars backed up at the bridge
before Pontaubault being one by one *searched* of all things!
you pulled up under the mitraillettes of four or five young
soldiers in that baggy battle dress, hardly any of them more
than boys, looking bored and manly, and a very good-looking
officer Hugh said was a para came to the car and saluted and
politely asked us to step out and might he see our pièces
d'identité, and while he did two more of his men went through
the car; and just on the far side of Pontaubault we found the
same sort of patrol was stopping traffic joining us from a road
on our left, from Alençon Hugh said, but we didn't find out
what was going on till in Dinan Hugh bought a paper, though
outside Dol we did see this huge DE GAULLE À L'ASILE—VIEUX
CINGLÉ daubed in red paint across the wall of an abandoned
stone barn.

I said to Hugh but to want to *assassinate* the poor man? but
he said why not?—they'd come within hours of pulling off a
military coup last year, and they'd have stood him up in front
of a firing squad if they had; been absolute touch-and-go as it

was. Because roughly speaking he said de Gaulle was the French equivalent of the kind of English landed gentry that went to Sandhurst and held the Empire together in the Guards, so, now, to the French army and navy and the landed families their officers came from, the General was simply a traitor to his country *and* his class; and when I said but over just Algeria or whatever? he said if you need pretexts you invent them—wasn't one of the slogans "Algérie Française"? One of the coup generals had even gone round proclaiming, "Ma passion pour mon sol natal me rend enragé!" foaming at the mouth to prove it, god what people.

—But for us to have got caught in anything so utterly un-likely—and so *French*-unlikely, heavens!—who would expect any of it? And from a man as old-régime-elegant as our beau Breton of a host above all!

Though from almost the first moment of that first day, even before lunch, I remember I thought there was a constraint about him one didn't somehow expect in such an ambience: why didn't he I wondered really properly introduce those men for instance, instead of just a wave of the hand and an easy phrase about his "local friends and colleagues." Of course the French can be very odd about mentioning names sometimes. But these men were so obviously out of place to pass for country neighbors or social equals, Hugh told me later they were so hard-eyed he'd taken them at first for off-duty police. And then, well, the *lunch* was so ordinary to give friends, just ray with black butter and then escalopes, wouldn't he I thought at least have a hunt board of some sort even if it wasn't that sort of a battue? so it was strange, bel homme or not.

We had lunch in a great wainscoted room he said had been the corps-de-garde originally, with one of those enormous Renaissance fireplaces, the coat-of-arms over it had its pranc-ing beasts gilded, and the quarterings in the field were enam-eled, azure and I guess it had been gules, but the wainscoting he said some eighteenth-century ancestor had added—even in summer the bare ashlar walls must have been bleak, so this aïeul had turned it into still another salon. But then it had been his own father who'd made a dining room of it, they'd no longer been using most of the château anyway, what could one do with nearly seventy rooms!—lambris dorés or not, one simply no longer found servants enough, so it was closed off, some of the attics he thought from Second Empire times. But the furniture surprised me—a beautiful dark-gleaming Hepplewhite dining table and shield-back chairs and a *pair* of serpentine-front sideboards with those banded inlays, and as we sat down I said to him how light and charming they made the room, what a pleasure to come on such English elegance in France, and he said he'd had an elegant Irish great-grandmother, these had been a part of her dowry.

And he was telling me more about her, he did make conversation beautifully, but those unexplained "friends" of his were just sitting humped over their plates at the other end of the table not even talking among themselves, from their faces not understanding even, and I thought *really* what people, not that I cared what they did or whether he was just having them eat with us because of the battue, but were we going through a whole meal like this? because goodness how awful, also how uncomfortable and silly, so I said to him, "Hugh and I, you know, do speak French, so why don't we, so much easier perhaps d'you think for your friends," so we did. But then they didn't take part in the conversation in French either, just sat feeding like lumps, staring sullenly down into their plates. Except of course now and then I could feel them sliding looks at me out of the corner of their unpleasant eyes the way that sort of men do, but who'd care.

Anyway, in French, naturally we were soon making conversation about the attempt to assassinate General de Gaulle, Hugh told about the "perquisitions" at Pontaubault, and I asked but why did everybody seem to expect these attentat people to hide out here in Brittany, when wasn't it Algeria they were in such a rage with the General about? One of the men at the end of the table muttered something, but Monsieur de Moëtland looked amused and said but madame where could any happy assassin of a French politician possibly be safer?—Bretons were *Celts* bon Dieu not Franks or Burgundians or Provençaux! Brittany wasn't even part of France for any true Breton—it was *occupied,* ces gredins de rois français had "annexed" it, by marrying Breton duchesses when they were helpless orphans: "Vous ne saviez vraiment pas, madame, que notre petite Duchesse Anne—" and on about Louis XII and François I and the young Duchesse Claude in 1514, tout le bazar, smiling into my eyes.

But I was hardly listening really, I was thinking *Mon Dieu qu'il est beau,* he's unbelievable, the skin of his neck is so white I feel as if I could taste it, and I wondered what he did for love. Because surely not I thought just some pretty peasant girl he'd have couche-toi-là, it had to be someone of his own class for such beauty, there's their endless talk about honor of course, but still. Because that head on your pillow, heavens! And I thought, if he were an American, by now I'd have begun to call him Alain, and even looking in his eyes what could I be but conscious of the rest of him, even his hands, so deft, gesturing, and I wondered how they would feel, touching me. But then Hugh must have said something, anyway I began listening again, and of all things they were discussing their *traditions....*

Or at least Alain was explaining about the Breton old-nobility, the only careers they could with honor follow were what they'd followed from Agincourt or before even, they became generals or admirals et voilà, what else was possible, and when Hugh said but not the Church too? he said laughing what battle-honors did a monseigneur or an abbé de cour get, and Hugh looked amused and said *his* family didn't go in for religion thank God either, just bibelot-collecting in a distinguished way and Main Line polo, and I thought goodness do I even know how I feel about either of them.

But also during all this I'd been noticing the surly-looking man across the table at the end more and more fidgeting, and looking hard at Alain, and now suddenly he scraped back his chair and stood up, and sort of blurted out, "Je m'excuse, monsieur le vicomte, mais vous savez . . . enfin . . . vu le boulot?" and the other three scrambled to their feet looking awkward too, and I wondered why he'd use a word like "job" for their battue; but all Alain said was, "Mais allez-y donc, sauvez-vous," hardly more than glancing down the table at them; so they mumbled *sieur-dame* the way they do, and slid their eyes at me a last time and went out, and the maid with them.

And then for a moment, it was no more than a wordless breath of time, the three of us sat there in one of those strange soft silences, like a transition between two worlds—as if from the tone one talks in when there are people there who aren't like us, to how we talk when there aren't. I mean we are brought up to say things in ways such people will understand, it saves time. And, really, their feelings I expect too. Because with them we *say* instead of just half-say with implications and references taken for granted that would make them see they were left out, anyhow now here was this sudden little silence, and I said to myself we are all three en pays de connaissance and thinking the same things about these men but won't say so, and this is what the silence is about.

But then Hugh broke it with a remark that showed it was something else too—though really he might have known Alain for years, the way he looked at him and said it—"I'm afraid our presence has put you in more of a difficulty than your good manners are letting show," and I thought, why, he's speaking English again, but what an odd thing to say, and I looked at Alain and then I saw something *was* the matter.

For a minute, though, he had such a strange uncertain expression that all I thought was he must think it's odd too; but then he sort of took a long breath, and turned to me looking unhappy and humble, and said, "The difficulty is, I have to tell you something, madame, and it distresses me to," and then he turned to Hugh again and said, "It's not quite the battue I've been giving you to understand," and I suppose I might have foreseen it all, right then.

Because the fact was, he said, simply these men were "separatists." Bretons had suffered under French rule for centuries, he was as good as a partisan of autonomy himself, he said, looking at me in a kind of apology, for really madame how not?—what Breton hadn't ancestors killed fighting them, c'était dans le sang to detest them! Did I know they still even refused to let Breton be used in Breton schools?—that outrageous piece of petty tyranny alone had turned Bretons by the thousands into fiery autonomists, and a few practically into maquisards! So, now, with these attempts on the General's life turning the police loose, anybody in any movement they could label "dissident" was being harassed, and these men in particular were understandably wary—two of them had been picked up already by the police after the earlier attentat, and roughly handled; so in short he had had he felt to assure them no possible word of their presence here would get out. *He* of course realized it wouldn't, from us, but—ah well, we saw the sort they were. And since now they did need a few hours to get safely off to another cachette, he found himself in the desolating necessity of asking us whether—

"Is what you're saying we *can't* leave?" Hugh said, and I thought but it's almost as if he'd been expecting it! and I was almost too surprised to think.

Simply it was a matter of the few remaining hours it would take, Alain said, to make arrangements, and get these men safely hors de portée somewhere else. Right or wrong, they felt *this* cachette had been rendered useless. What he was asking us was to have the indulgence, the vraie gentillesse, he said almost pleadingly, to give him the pleasure of having us under his roof meantime.

Then nobody said anything.

But I thought *really* what an unbelievable conversation!—this drawing-room punctilio and politesse when are we or *aren't* we in something rather unpleasant? *And* odd!

So I said but heavens—well *somebody* had to say something!—I said but weren't his sympathies known? he being "pays" after all, wasn't he? because his lovely château I meant I'd have thought would have been one of the first places a police "rafle" closed in on. But he said ah but madame a "sweep" through a paysage touffu like this they knew would be hopeless, in Basse Bretagne every second field disappeared into woods or hedgerows, Dieu might have made the landscape exprès to hide in: no, the police would spot-check, and more or less at random. Hugh said mildly by "random" he supposed he meant "with luck"? but he said why not?—with the château's seventy-odd rooms *and* attics and cellars a handful of men no more than these could vanish at a minute's warning, there were even three or four—wasn't "priests' holes" the English for it? in the thicknesses of chimney walls, from Chouan times.

Hugh sort of looked at him, and even I thought "warning"? with the lodge gates wide open and no concierge? ... But then Hugh decided to say it anyway: what if, that morning, it had happened to be a police scout car l'intrus, not us? and of course what was there to say.

So Alain just made this sort of rueful face and said ah well, his friends hadn't, he admitted, "pris leurs dispositions" very efficiently, in fact they'd been offhand to the point of folly, he threw up his hands at them; but what was inexcusable—and past all apology, he said humbly, looking at me—was the vexation, the contrariété impardonnable, to madame above all, of what had occurred; and I remember thinking but can he actually be helpless or something about these men? and I looked at Hugh.

But he might have been no more than amused!—he said to Alain, "You mean these nervous friends of yours shouldn't have let us find them with their mitraillettes showing?" as if it were a joke. But Alain looked so nonplussed for a moment, by the irony or whatever, that Hugh must have decided to make it plain, anyway he added, "In other words all this is just our bad luck?"

I thought, what is going to happen. Because now Hugh was looking at him with no expression at all, and I said to myself but a fiery animal like *Hugh?* . . . But then after a moment he said in a perfectly amiable tone, "You damn' well wouldn't put up with this yourself, why under the sun d'you think I will?"—really it might merely have been some bantering argument they were having! And Alain answered in practically the identical easy tone, "Mais si à ma place c'était vous le responsable?" But he'd I thought flushed just a little saying it, and why had he gone back to French? and Hugh looked as if he were thinking oh nonsense too, and said, "You can't seriously think these people are in *danger* dammit?" and suddenly Alain did flush, and said in a sort of haughty voice, "Il ne s'agit pas, monsieur, de ce qu'on pense—j'ai donne ma parole!"

Hugh said to me later, "I damn' near asked him flat how in God's papist name he'd ever let himself get trapped in anything as simple as high-mindedness—god I was exasperated!" but all he looked was sort of politely sardonic, and he said, "L'avantageux de la vérité est qu'elle a un cachet," and the maid brought in the coffee, and at least it was a transition, for all of us.

Anyhow if Hugh wasn't disturbed why should I be? Also if this was an outrage, Alain was the one to be upset about it, not Hugh or I, but *this* was not the moment to discuss it! so quite simply I said to Alain what lovely old gardens it looked as if he had, the meadows beyond all golden with gorse in flower, and the ferny fronds of—was it bracken? and the green headland above the sea; so presently we walked there.

And he began to apologize all over again after a little, he was totally *dejected*, he said, not just at the inconvenance but what must we think of a loyalty to a cause we'd never heard of, loyalty it *was* but then what it was subjecting us to! could we forgive it *or* him for that?—forgive even (he begged me) to the point of considering coming back some day soon under happier circumstances? So I said but where really had we intended to go in particular anyway? so why not; also he couldn't have made us feel more en pays de connaissance if we'd known him already, I'd almost begun wondering what I should call him, I said, and I suppose my eyes did caress him a little—well, he was beautiful, heavens!—though I said of course first names between us ah *this* soon would be so unheard-of un-French I thought we shouldn't try to cross that particular cultural frontier quite yet, even if we weren't perhaps entirely thinking of each other as monsieur and madame. And I thought if Hugh weren't here what would he do? and I said to myself shall I charm him and see?—at least the theory of it? I have to pass the time *somehow* and amuse myself don't I? so all the long lazy afternoon I sort of did, and we had tea by the carp pool and fed crumbs to the huge old carp, and by the time we went in I could almost have laughed, he was so uneasy about me already.

Because all this talk about honor, heavens! when I thought what if really I have only to stretch out my hand for him, wife of his guest or not? oh mon pauvre Alain how mean I could so easily be to you, I could be absolutely pétrie de méchanceté, goodness what lovely fun, shall I, or shall I? Especially since Hugh had spotted how things were too.

And what arrogance, was just *amused!* We'd come up to our room to change for dinner, I was at the pier glass tiffing my hair, and he came up behind me and took my waist in his fingers and said, "What are your angel plans for this helpless viscount?" brushing his lips softly down my neck and along into the hollow of my shoulder. I said, "What ever made you

think you were supposed to have noticed?" and wriggled, but
he snorted that scoffing way he does and said, "You and your
blue-eyed apostasies!" and held me. So naturally I said, "You
don't really think *this* is an ambience I'd have picked, do you?
—for an affair with you either!" Because "apostasy" anyway!
From *him!* I said, "You're mussing me," and he said, "But to
my taste," snickering, and he let me go and we went down to
dinner. And thank goodness those men—the surly one in particular: Hugh said later he thought he was a Belgian, an un-
reconstructed Rexist even, from wartime—anyway thank
goodness none of them were there. And Alain didn't bother to
explain why. Also it was a *good* dinner—beautiful pink heaps
of cold langoustines with mayonnaise, then tournedos with a
lovely glaze with rounds of marrow and artichoke hearts, and
for dessert a mont-blanc aux marrons, and the wines astonishing, I suppose they always are when one first gets back to
France again, but these *were*, and we must have dawdled over
the cheese and the fruit and the coffee and the calvados till
well on toward eleven, and in such a lovely haze I had to be
careful how I let Alain look at me, I didn't even want to go
out for a minute in the moonlight before bed I was so sleepy
and delicious.

And then it was so amusing, there was no electricity except
downstairs—how long had it been, I said to Hugh, since he or
I had gone up to bed by candlelight!—so charming, too, when
we'd lit the two oil chimney-lamps the maid had left for us on
the coiffeuse, the bedroom all shadows and soft dusk and the
tall curtains drawn against the night and the bed properly
turned down, even a brass bidon à goulot of hot water by the
washstand—a century mightn't have passed, Hugh said, it was
so tranquil, so unchanged, did I feel like my pantalooned great-
grandmother? I said then hadn't he better test the bed? He said
for softness or for feed? and bounced. I asked, "Rather hard?"
and he said, "Hair mattress," and made a face. But that wasn't
what our minds were on, and presently he came over behind

me as I was finishing my face for the night at the coiffeuse, and our eyes met in the glass and he said, "What a thing."

I hadn't decided whether or not I'd begun to feel a little cross, or about what, so I said, "Why on earth did it have to occur to you to say I was your *wife*."

He said, "Whose damn' business if you're not?"

"But so stuffy don't you think, Hugh darling!"

He smirked at me in the glass and slid his hand affectionately down into my nightgown and said, "Turning out perfectly agreeable this way isn't it?"

As of course it was; so I wrinkled my nose at him and said, "You mean here I anyway am, sharing that rather hard bed with a wicked cousin instead of not?"

He said, "I do what thank God I'm wickedly tempted to"— and there in the glass we were, faintly smiling conspirators, the long lovely night waiting to close us round still one time more.

—Except later it was, much later I guess it could have been by then, I'd thought he was asleep, and I nearly was, lying there all drowsy-warm and close, hardly thinking of anything but the feel of him all through me still, all the lingering luxury, heaven what a thing it can be when they are like this, and the memory of how, and half-dozing I wondered d'you suppose he was like this with Georgie? though then of course I thought but how could he have been, so young. And only with *her* anyhow! Though I wonder what he would say if I asked him —except hoh! would he even remember! So then I thought why not have a conversation-in-my-mind with him, I could for instance use an amused coaxing voice and just say darling what was Georgie, you know, *like?* so then he might yawn and say what's anybody like, and I'd say I don't mean just in bed, I mean her—her— But how would I say it to him? her "taste in men"? because imagine, after *him*, marrying a man she could call "Petchie"! oh the poor silly, and then that first time she was unfaithful to him bleating, "But I thought I'd feel *weird!*"

to me afterwards. . . . Or no; I'd say Hugh darling why don't you ever tell me about your women, I tell you about my men, what *they* do, I'd say, kissing his throat, do you make us over to your specifications while you have us? or do different ones of us just have different impressions of you, and maybe feelings about you too, because our effects on you differ? and I was wondering how much perhaps did we when suddenly he sort of lazily stretched all along against me and shifted the arm that was under me, and said yawning, "You believe this honnête-homme account of his?"—wide *awake!* I thought how absolutely so soon *can* they forget how we must still feel, heavens! but I said, ". . . What account, darling," trying to think.

He said, "This host of ours's, what d'ye suppose? About these 'separatists.' You believe it?"

I thought why shouldn't I have? but I said, "Oughtn't I to?"

"You took those mitraillettes for costume drama or something? With for God's sake the safeties off?"

I said goodness, were they? but how strange, I supposed I hadn't thought (and I guess really of course I hadn't)—just I said I'd wondered, at lunch, why if these men were the vicomte's friends they didn't more seem to be. Or at ease even.

He snorted, and said good *god*—hard-eyed Paris underworld thugs like these in the back-nowhere of *Brittany* and I hadn't wondered? Or wondered what this seigneurial host of ours was giving them asylum for? Hiding political dissidents, d'accord; because the police were picking up anybody and everybody, parfait. But a national manhunt for assassins was hardly a danger for mere *dissidents*. If the police picked them up they'd be knocked about a little, and held a day or so, and turned loose. "But suppose, my angel," he said, "suppose part of the gang *is* what they are—had you thought of *that* explanation? With this helplessly honorable viscount now in it over his head entirely?"

I thought *Alain?. . . .* I was appalled, and I said, "Oh Hugh *no!*"

"Hasn't he as good as told us where he stands?" he said. "Simply loyalty to what his race and his upright heritage tell him to do! Only, unluckily, the danger of honor is, it puts you at the mercy of extremists. So here he is, involved with *these* people!"

And what could I do but see it. I said, "Oh Hugh how awful."

"And some of the kind of men behind them very likely old fellow-officers of his into the bargain," he said, sort of grimly, "or cadets with him at Saint-Cyr," and when I said, "But Hugh you sound *upset* for him?" he said, "Well, dammit, I am!"

So we lay there.

But then I said, "But you looked as if you *believed* what he told us about it."

Why not? he said—there was no danger. It was a damn' quick-witted and plausible scenario: why should they think a stray couple of touring American innocents didn't believe what they were entertainingly told? It was seeming *not* to would have been the danger. And what would I suggest he shoot our way out with then?

So why *not* give this entirely presentable viscount the pleasure of our company he asked for?—had the impoverished old-nobility so often, on sight, begged me to stay the weekend that I hadn't even a civilized curiosity about their amenities? Bed hard or not, he added, and stroked me.

But then, ah well, he went on, everybody was stupid, yes, only did the privileged classes have to be stupid so often too? —people who simply didn't seem to realize they were still going on being their ancestors? It wasn't dammit that he didn't sympathize (what after all did *he* do!) but good god could there be unlikelier unlikenesses? *Us*, for instance, and that oaf of an ancestor who'd landed in Philadelphia in the 1680s—

what genetic fraction of *my* elegant ninth-generation body and
man-beguiling soul was Wiltshire yeoman? Why, I wouldn't so
much as know what to make light conversation with the old
guy about if I met him. And de Moëtland went back *five* and a
half centuries, to Agincourt! There wouldn't be even a
drawing-room pronunciation in common! Yet now *that* one-nth
ancestral genetic fraction was exactly the folly that had him on
the absolute blind brink of catastrophe. . . .

I said, "Such a rhetorical darling, aren't you," but as I went
to sleep I wondered whether I *should* perhaps be a little upset
about Alain.

But in the morning we went swimming—sunbathing, anyway: the water was *cold;* and then at lunch Alain asked
whether it would perhaps amuse us to see some of the long-
disused part of the château?—there was a ballroom for instance that had considerable period charm, originally it had
been the great hall and still had one of those huge baronial
fireplaces at each end, with stone sockets for flambeaux, but in
Louis XV's time it had been made into a ballroom in the best
Louis XV taste, would it at all help divert us if he showed us
through? and naturally I said how lovely, but Hugh said two
of the château's exterior façades had rather taken his eye,
some of the architectural detail was remarkable, in fact it was
the sort of thing that brought out the Piranesi in him, so would
we forgive him, he said, looking blandly at me, if he wandered
about outside and sketched instead?—and I almost laughed
aloud, he knew exactly what I'd think of doing, and what
other man would have had the arrogance to turn me loose to
do it! ("Arrogance my eye," he said that night, "Just scientific
curiosity." But it *was*.)

So after lunch out he sauntered with his sketching pad, and
Alain and I began our tour. The ballroom first, and he was
right: even dusky and long-disused it was enchanting, a long
tall room all white-and-gold rococo lambrissage, and when the
myriads of candles in the great lustres were lit it must have

been as gay as it was magnificent, though alas Alain said they hadn't been lit in many years, not since the wedding of a young cousine of his, long before the war, it was the first ball he'd ever seen, he was a small boy, he'd been absolutely ébahi, *stunned* practically, by the white brilliance of the dresses of waltzing girls and the glitter of their partners' uniforms—and the lovely child, he now remembered, had died in childbirth before the year had gone.

Beyond, there was a graceful oval antechamber, with white-and-gold paneling too, but then the reception rooms that opened off it on the other three sides had waxed wainscoting instead, beautiful dark boiseries with fielded panels in the English style, and bead-and-ovolo moldings instead of rococo, the beading delicately gilded, and glints of gilding in the cornices too and in the course of guilloches under them— *lovely*, and in these rooms the furniture was very good Louis XV or XVI though it needn't have come from Paris. But there *was* mostly provincial furniture in the salons in the wing Alain took me to next, the wing he lived in, some of it even that awful Renaissance stuff, and here the lambrissage was much simpler, even severe—plain bolection moldings, applied, or that tiresome linenfold paneling, with battens or astragals, and in the large salon simply tapestries instead, faded really the color of mildewed porridge, huge ghastly classical scenes that must have begun fading in Bourbon times.

But then, as we wandered on, and up this stairway or that to other floors, all was stone. And a *feeling* of the silence, as if it were something hooded and softly waiting, at the end of a curving passageway, or in some dusty cul-de-sac a voice had perhaps not echoed in for a hundred years, lost to everything but the scuffling of a squirrel across the floors of deserted rooms. Or at the end of some dim corridor we would come on a turret stair winding up around the worn stone of its newel, and climb to a tower chamber where the slow dusts had settled so feathery fine our shoes left prints where we crossed to peer from a window down, if only to see what side of the endless maze we had come out on, and once I found I was looking down into a little interior courtyard I never did work out the position of, oh it was a kind of utterly charming dust-and-desolation everywhere I told Alain, but goodness what a place to look after! and he said yes even the bare *detail*—did I know there had had to be one man who did nothing except lug wood twelve hours a day for the fires? ...

Sometimes in the long enchanted afternoon a room would have a history he'd tell me, he'd been no more than five or six when his grandfather had begun making him learn the château's history by heart, practically room by room, then when he'd grown he'd of course found out about amusing scandals as well, two of his eighteenth-century ancestresses seemed to have been particularly light-minded—one of them had even had a *Huguenot* lover as an added flippancy! perhaps the ancestor she was married to had been a bit stuffier a dévot than the average run. Or she'd just been plantée là in deepest Brittany a little longer than a pretty woman's vanity would put up with, who could say; and then there was the impassioned Vicomtesse Aurélie, whose husband unluckily ran her lover through the heart and killed him—that very day she'd got the fallen man's sword from his second, knotted her scarf around the hilt, plunged it to the cross-guard into the mattress of her husband's bed, ordered up her calèche and her groom, and vanished. Myth if one liked, he said happily; myth possibly also that she'd vanished a second time, and for good, into Russia, in the coach of Catherine the Great's ambassador. But not to believe in selected myth of one's heritage would hardly be good manners, didn't I believe in mine? and of course I said heavens yes: I couldn't after all very well say they *were* rather less simpleminded.

And from some of the rooms, bare and deep in dust or not, what views there were out over the sunlit sea, we stood at one and I said could it always did he suppose have seemed as lovely and by itself as this? such long centuries on this shining headland, with the depths of the beechwood behind like a green wall against the intrusions of the world—the landscape might have lain here dreaming and unchanged for a thousand years, from didn't they call it "the long peace of Henry I"? people going on pilgrimages slowly everywhere, and perhaps abbeys too were founded in those remote valleys to rediscover the wonder of being alone. . . .

He said in an uncertain voice but "the wonder"?—was he to believe that *I* could wish to be alone? and I looked into his blue eyes and thought, As if either of us were made to be anything ever but à deux! but I said, softly, but ah hadn't he, too, moments to be alone to himself in?—to withdraw out of time, the time that goes hour by hour by hour, into one's own space and frame of time, where one saw things one had done not as one felt about them as one did them but as if they were history, seeing it all, I meant, in the real time of memory; but I thought, heavens I'll confuse him, so I said maybe this was why his ancestors had stayed here those centuries, to be alone, and I turned to the window again and added, gently, maybe that was why he did too.

And, waiting, I thought how still it was in those ancient rooms, the sunlight fell through the dusty panes like a pattern of pale tiles across the bare brown oak of the floor, or hung like a haze of gold, sifting motes slowly revolving, as if in that unstirring air of years even our silence, our caught breath, were a motion somehow. I was turned gazing off and away over the flowering headland and the blue sea far out as if forever, and Alain was so close now at my shoulder I felt the warmth of his breath flutter the hair over my ear, and in the middle of a phrase his voice had stopped. I thought, *Now?* . . . and certainly the air about us was charged with that lovely electricity, I could almost feel him trembling, and I waited. Except then I began to think is his arrogance as different from

Hugh's as this? so I turned, so near now I heard the thudding of his heart, and I let my eyes say *Here then I am?* . . .

So of course how could he stand it, he was like a steel spring as it was, wild, I thought but really can no woman ever have done quite *this* to him? goodness how agreeable—and he did do his honnête-homme best not to, he stammered something desperately light about ". . . your eyes' soft threat," I remember wondering what the French for it would be, ah but his face was absolutely agonized, he was lost, so all I had to say was, "But you must see I cannot mon cher listen to such things, how can I honorably, I mustn't, to such disturbing sweetness," in oh how soft a voice, and he gave up— "J'en suis comme transpercé!" he said in his throat, and something choky about de part en part le corps, and simply, well, *grabbed* me, and bent my head back kissing me, and when I twisted my face away kissed my throat, just as violently, and my neck and the curve of my shoulder, and my earring fell off.

I thought goodness d'you suppose this is the sort of mauling makes French women swoon? what verb would they I wonder use, se rendre?—or no, céder's better: that's it, on cède. Except I thought but *I* don't, mon petit vicomte, tu es beau comme le jour, but making love is not a biological confrontation, how can you know so little, oh have been *taught* so little, you are probably the most beautiful bel homme I shall ever lay eyes on *and* a charmer but I am not here to be manhandled for your instruction.

Still, by this time it was beginning to come to him that I wasn't swooning or doing in fact anything but wait to be let go, so after a little more I gently took myself out of his arms. But I touched his cheek with the tips of my fingers for an instant, and murmured, "You are unsettlingly sweet, ah how you are! but mon ami I—I—" and left it unfinished so as not to seem heartless or unmoved. Or have him feel just rejected. Though with nobody to see, what matter, heavens. So of course then he took me in his arms again, trembling, this time, and I put my forehead down against his shoulder and for a little while let him. As Hugh says, if love is a duel it ought to enjoy at least the courtesies of eighteenth-century rules.

But then at last I had to say, "But mon très doux Alain I do you know happen to be the wife of a man who's your guest," and I lifted my head and kissed his cheek, *really* what I do and what I'm doing it's *wild* how different! and then I said, "Now please will you let me go," and he did, looking so shaken I half-repented. Oh but what incantations I've recited to myself sometimes afterwards, as reason or excuse, or as mere good manners. Or just as emotional décor. Hugh said once I was a matter of style. And I am.

But then of course there was the rest of the day and the evening to be got through as if nothing had happened, and the proprieties reactivated, and I was glad when at dinner Hugh said he couldn't remember when *he*'d had two pleas-anter days, circumstances or no circumstances, but now he really thought we'd given Alain's friends head start enough, wouldn't he agree?—tomorrow morning would make it forty-eight hours, he'd not noticed any of the men around any longer except that Belgian or whatever he was, so after break-fast we'd say what he hoped Alain too would feel might be only au revoir, and be on our way—"and with proper direc-tions this time!" and Alain said steadily, without looking at me, that alas he supposed he'd no right to keep us, much as he'd like to; and so next morning after breakfast we packed, and Hugh and the man took our bags down, and in a little I followed.

The brilliance of summer morning was over everything, such a dazzle of light it half-blinded me as I came out of the château into it with the maid and my dressing case—sun hot on the gardens and the headland, and the sea like blue haze off and off beyond, and I was just crossing the terrasse to the broad stair down to the courtyard, thinking what loveliness, what country peacefulness, almost I wish we were staying on, when I heard this sort of snarling shout, "Eh, halte-là, le copain! Laissez!" and I came to the balustrade and there at the foot of the stair Hugh was standing, hatless in the towering light, by the open trunk of his car, our suitcases lined up on the cobbles beside him, and sprinting across toward him from the corner of the château was that surly brute of a Belgian with his mitraillette pointed straight at him. Hugh must have been bending over into the trunk shifting things to make room for our suitcases, and had just straightened up and turned, anyway he had a tire iron in his hand, or maybe it was the jack handle, and he sort of balanced it, and the man stopped fifteen feet away and snapped, "Essayez pas de coup, hein?" and at my shoulder I heard the maid gasp something very scared, I suppose in Breton, and then for a long moment Hugh and the man just stood there in the sun, the breadth of the stair-foot between them, rigid, each by the stone newel his side, poised as motionless as if time had stopped; and then suddenly I saw Hugh just very gently heft the tire iron, and I said, *"Hugh, don't!"*

His head jerked around up toward me, startled, and he looked at me as if I were a child who'd said something absolutely mannerless; but then his face relaxed, and he said almost banteringly, "You want to bet on it?" and I said to the maid, "Allez vite *vite* chercher Monsieur," and she scuttered back into the château wailing, and I saw Hugh turn toward the man again and oh god I thought how can I stop him, stop either of them, is this insane thing going to just go ahead and *happen?* and all I could seem to do was think *oh please please* so hard I almost wasn't sure I wasn't saying it aloud.

But then next moment here *did* come Alain out of the château at a dead run, he must have been on his way to see us off and nearly there already anyhow, and he sprinted across the terrasse to where I stood at the top of the stair and burst into such an absolute fury of rapid French down at the man that really I didn't understand a word.

The man didn't even look up at him, just sort of drawled out, "And *my* neck if they take off, mon beau commandant? . . ." as if he were talking to a child.

Alain said, in a voice of steel, "Je vous le repète—monsieur m'en a donné sa parole!"

The man said contemptuously, "Et puis après?" not taking his eyes from Hugh.

Alain went as white as if he'd been struck. He cried, "Vous vous *rangerez*, nom de Dieu!" and plunged down the stair two steps at a time straight at him, and out of the corner of my eye suddenly I saw Hugh starting toward him too and I thought *and I am here helpless.* The man had sprung back two or three steps away from the newel and spun round facing Alain, flinging up his mitraillette and shouting, "Halte-là—*halte!*" terrified, and as Alain reached the foot of the stair he—I *heard* that awful sort of multiple thudding!—he fired this *full burst* from his gun point-blank into Alain's poor breast, it knocked him straight over backwards onto the bottom steps of the stair as if he'd been picked up and slammed there, and just that instant too late Hugh smashed his tire iron or whatever it was into the man's crazed shouting-open face and sent him catapulting back headfirst over one of the mounting-blocks and down on the other side, the mitraillette clattering out of his hands onto the cobbles, and as I ran horrified down the stair to where Alain's body had begun to slump and roll I saw Hugh spring up onto the block and look down with his arm up to strike again, though then I saw his shoulder relax, and then I was on my knees by Alain.

He'd nearly rolled off the bottom step, he was face down and blood was absolutely welling out from under him, little scarlet rivulets of it running into the cracks of the cobbles and turning dark and thick in the dust between, and I thought but if I turn him over and find that beautiful head *too* has been . . .? And I supposed I ought to try to turn him over but I felt too half-sick to, and anyway I heard Hugh coming back across to me and then he was looming over me saying, "He's *dead?*" in a shocked voice, and I said, "Yes. Yes, he is," like conversation in a dream, and I looked up at him, the sun blazing down on his uncovered head so white-hot gold his face almost seemed deep in shadow, his hand was sort of clenching and unclenching the tire iron as if he couldn't make up his mind what to do with it, and he said with distaste, "I may have hit the other one too hard," and then for a long moment there in the sunblaze around us the world was as summer-morning still as if there had never been sound.

I said, rather wildly I expect, "Will you put that thing *down?*" but he'd turned and was calling up to the maid, she was leaning weakly against one of the urn'd newels at the top of the stair balustrade, she was making gagging noises and when Hugh snapped at her, "Mais filez donc!—téléphonez à la police, nom de Dieu!" I thought she was going into hysterics. But then Hugh saw, and softened his tone—*soyez une brave fille* and *du courage, hein?* and so forth, and she was to get the doctor here at *once*, would she?—and after just a little, softly weeping, she ran obediently back into the château, and Hugh went across to the mounting-block and looked down over. But right away he turned back toward me, making a face, and looked round for the mitraillette, and I must have said, "Fingerprints" or something, because I remember he said, "Not that a doctor'll matter much either," but he dropped the tire iron by the gun; and then what did he do but come back across and kneel down by me and pick up my hand and turn it gently over and put his lips to my palm. For just that moment. The sun on his hair. Then he looked up at me and said, ". . . if you know why the hell I am doing this," and I thought *against the awfulness, really*, but I said, "One has to do something," except suddenly I was seeing him so differently, how had he done what he had done, the sheer bursting violence of him, and the speed of it, yet now *this* look, and he was saying, "Are you all right?" and it was all such horrifying confusion and shock, and I heard myself saying, "Oughtn't we to turn him over?" and him saying, "You've got blood on your skirt" as if that were an answer.

But I said, "His poor face is in the *dust*, Hugh!" and he said, "Get back a little, then," and I did. But of course, because of the bottom step, he had to turn him right into the wet pool of his blood and for a moment I thought I couldn't look. But then of course I did, and I suppose moving him made more blood gulp out soaking still, the stain seemed to spread out farther over his poor bullet-slashed shirt before our eyes, it was horrible, I thought shall I ever again remember *anything* in such savage detail? but his face was unscathed.

And his blue eyes through those long dark-gold lashes were half open, he might almost I thought if I moved into the line of their vision be looking at me still, even if only the way people do in delirium, glazed over sort of; but to look and *not* see? not to *be* there to see?—though what explanation is death I thought either, and I said to Hugh, "Shouldn't we close his eyes?" Though then when I reached out over to, I felt the sun strike hot on the back of my hand and I wondered would his eyelids be—well, still warm? but then I thought how silly, and stretched out my hand and saw its shadow fall across his face and then down over that empty gaze, and when my palm touched his forehead of course it was sun-warm too; and I said to myself I am closing a dead lover's eyes.

I don't quite remember what happened for a little after that. I knelt there. Then there was a clatter I remember of wooden clogs across the terrasse, and the houseman appeared at the top of the stair looking out of his mind and clutching a shotgun and Hugh was a time calming him down; but then he came and looked at Alain from a little distance and crossed himself, and his lips moved, praying. But then Hugh sent him off at a run to the lodge to see the gates were open for the police, and sat down at the top of the stairs and said, "You just going to sit there?" and I said, "Kneel," and he said, mildly, "Kneel there, then?" and I thought oh Hugh darling let us alone, all three of us, Hugh, until I can decide whether I knew him much either.

Because listen, I said to him in my mind: as in girlhood I knew the wild weeds, but by their sprays in the summer dusk, Hugh, not their names, so, now, whom must I think I know except as they seem to me? even a lover is an ally against loneliness who still hasn't claim enough to encroach upon my solitude for me to "know." Is there some *rule* one has to, about men?—except for perhaps convenience, I wanted to say to him, sitting there so long-familiar and easy against the lichened scrollings of the balustrade, the sun in those cocksure libertine eyes, gazing down at me but perhaps a little through me too, though at what, I am not sure I shall ever be quite certain again.

Ah though, really, I thought, I might almost not be a part of any of this, and not horrified or in this strange grief for whatever it is, as if all this were somehow no more than a tiny scene painted on crystal and I were here merely to tell you how brittle and quick to shatter it is, this scene how can anyone civilized ever explain—the château on its low headland above the sea, the blaze of morning over the gardens, and I kneeling here on the cobbles, waiting, an edge of the bartizan's shadow just touching the fingers of my hand; and ah how peaceful, how wordless-still my lovers, in the long murmur of this day, Hugh who since this is France is mon amant, and Alain who—ah, well, might have gone gallantly back to being some other woman's I suppose really, poor French darling, and I *me* between them; and I remember I had just noticed that the slow, still-mortal spreading of the red stain through his shirt had stopped, when Hugh said, "Why did you come with me?" and I had to think of something to reply.

THREE

A FEW FINAL DATA DURING THE FUNERAL

Searching the cave gallery of your face
My torch meets fresco after fresco
                    —Empson

A proper upbringing being what it is, I can't say I had expected to set out for a memorial service to my oldest friend—even now a long month dead—after a night in the arms of his eighth-or-ninth-from-the-last ex-girl, but then beautiful Camilla had always been a woman of sentiment.

Drowsily murmuring now, in our contented night, "Sweet Simon were you surprised? . . ." though obviously it was by then many hours too late to be.

". . . and abashed?"—unquestions ending in a bland "But think if we'd known *then!* . . ." the flutter of soft breath in my ear just not quite a giggle.

A dreamy pause.

As of an angel musing.

On what, however, turned out to be the indecorums of feminine reminiscence: "Sweetie you'd never *guess* what he'd do sometimes . . ."—mildly scatological particulars; little splutters of ladylike ribaldry at the comedy she made of it—". . . like some *navvy*, Simon—imagine!"

A pause.

"Though goodness what a time to tell such things!"

Pause.

"Though *sweet* Simon how unbosoming we do seem to've become, goodness!" a knee sliding its silky flattery between mine; and so, in tranquil posthumous infidelity, off to sleep.

I too, shortly.

After having decently wondered, for a moment, as one marauding male about another, whether Hugh's ghost mightn't, just conceivably, in the circumstances, be walking.

Here and now. In the felicities of *this* nth-from-the-last ex-bedroom.

But Hugh a bystander?—ghost or not? It would be wildly out of character. Theologically speaking, anyhow, why should he leave those flowery retinues of girls about him in Elysium? Girls in love were an appanage of his immortality his libertine's eye hardly even dissembled when he painted them. Why, this sleek and sleeping armful here of mine you can gaze at, any day, on her wall in the Corcoran, and observe (and be right) that though she's painted in the pose of Michelangelo's Erythrean Sibyl, a hallowed sibyl is hardly what you'd conclude the painter knew her as, nor is the way the paint's put on a bystander's.

So, just in case, I muttered an avaunt: Ghost of my lifelong friend, old unbystanding Hugh, have the Philadelphia decency to be gone! Take to your spectral heart those opening eloquences of the *Corriere della Sera*'s Non starà più a contemplarci obituary: "The great distinguished head is to look upon us no more." Unhaunt us, Hugh—bless us like a gent, and back to the hypotheses of Eternity.

Mind you, canvases or girls—and deplored or not—Hugh Tatnall's is a renown he was entitled to. Even if for nothing else, that arrogant rake's persona of his stood for something through an era when the intellectual ambience in fashion had been a wincing and haggard self-pity at the eliot prospects of the soul. Not for Hugh: *his* subject was the landscapes and still lifes of Man's and his own individuated rut. Very reassuring, too—being after all how we had all behaved (and approved of behaving) before the psychagonists and the education-mongers explained it all away. For Hugh still did behave that way: as a high-church critic who detested him put it, "Even Tatnall's madonnas, if the appalling fellow had ever painted any, would look as if they'd just got out of bed with him!"

(A baffling observation. Not only did he paint madonnas—

in the years he amused himself being artist-sometimes-in-residence at Smith he did a series of them. They were, I admit, from the light-minded side of him. Parody amused him: Manet's *Olympia*, he used to say, was a quotation of Titian's *Venus of Urbino*, so why shouldn't he "quote" Raphael's madonnas? They were jeux d'esprit, to be given to his friends rather than exhibited. I own two of them myself, including his enchanting Nadezhda, *The Virgin as Bona Dea*, and many of the rest of them are at Smith too. All the models were, after all, Smith girls. And if they all look as if they have just been in bed with him, why not? They all had.)

Now this famous old charmer of a rake was gone.

And famous now not least, a Sophoclean chorus would have chanted at you, for the manner of his death. For Hugh had been shot down point-blank by an overwrought young Pisana in the most newsworthy sexual circumstances.

European newspapers had been fond of him for years, Italian especially. He spent nearly half his time in Italy; he was known there widely; his work was known. He even made news for them—the academic uproar he'd caused, for instance, the time he made Dante the subject of an hilarious fresco he painted on the ceiling of La Buonabolgia, the nightclub of a local friend of his: there were outraged cries of everything from enormità to bambineria. ("What the devil are they fussing about?" he complained. "Composition's impeccable—it's Rubens's sketch for his *Apotheosis of the Duke of Buckingham* practically to the square inch. . . .") Even his airport interviews sold papers: if nothing else, he was always good for an off-the-cuff analysis of la ragazza americana, that year's illustrative specimen on his arm for the photographers. And now, alas, it was almost as journalistically natural as it was sadly final: there he lay dead in Italy under Paris *Herald* headlines.

I read them, at breakfast, in Grenoble, at a United Nations conference on the Humanities. I had been agreeably laying siege (in French: a bit cramping) to a dreamy-eyed young instructress in semasiology from Bucharest. With a heavy heart I raised the siege, packed my bag, hopped a plane across the Alps, and was in Florence even before our cultural attaché got in from Rome.

Hugh had inherited, from an expatriate uncle, a late-Baroque palazzo, off the Vicolo Saltimbeni. He had been letting half the piano nobile, most recently to an aging marchesa, a years-past gallantry it seems of his uncle's; the rest he kept as a pied-à-terre. And, of course, studio: nothing like Tuscan light, he said, to mold the contours of a pretty bottom or crotch. I found the quarter an anthill of reporters: news must have been phenomenally short. Even the *Economist* and *Le Monde* stringers showed up. When they discovered that I was Hugh's executor, they went into happy mass-production: for days, headlines were black and exclamatory with every scabrous invention the quarter could come up with. In Italy, tutto si sa—it is the inviolably clandestine, your midnight secrets known only to God, that are on your every neighbor's tongue.

(I might as well have stayed on in Grenoble a day or so. The Dacian accent in French is delicious. So had been the tactics: surely un si beau classiciste should remember that Dacia had held out against the Roman Empire itself for three whole centuries—"et vous voulez qu'on cède à un simple colon au bout d'autant de jours? . . .")

—Hugh had spent late winter and the cold Tuscan spring in Florence. The Smith girl with him this time was an Art-and-Architecture major conveniently doing her departmental junior-year-abroad; her name was Persis Dove. She was very serious-minded. But also she was satiny and sweetly shaped, a slender pale-gold blonde with great green eyes and an enchanting voice, a voice that absolutely caressed you, and to complete her amenities Hugh had been teaching her to cook.

But by grotesquely bad luck Persis had met a rinnovatrice at the Uffizi, a girl in her late twenties named Francesca. She was a talented but also a moody painter, who hardly ever sold a canvas: in effect she was working as a restorer full time. She was a tall, tawny-haired, rather smoldering Pisan, with one of those stylized angular bodies, and a kind of fiery chic. And she wanted to improve her English. And didn't Persis need—*ma sul serio*, need!—a great deal more practice in Italian? So the two of them had been instructively exchanging language lessons as spring came on.

But ahimè, language is not parts of speech alone. *Miri la bocca*, Ariosto's sonnet exhorts you, that mouth

Which sweet the smile hath as sweet word it speaketh.

As spring came on, enchantment came on too.

"Because oh *dear*," Persis mourned to me (in that soft voice that made every word she spoke sound as if she were about to breathe *oh my darling love* at you), "one day Francesca began, well, courting me! And naturally I— Well, we were 'a tu per tu,' isn't that what they say? though that doesn't *mean* that, does it?—except, well, it was an aspect of my sexuality I hadn't known, I mean she made me aware, Professor Shipley! I don't mean I wasn't Hugh's all the time, but she began to court me and after a while, well, Hugh *saw*. And he refused to have her in, even! Except when we had her stupid husband too, for drinks, or there'd be this meal Hugh felt like showing off his cooking with, he used to say Toulouse-Lautrec was a chef too, wasn't he? so it was all just horrid and mixing-up—and *dreadful* at first, Francesca was so furiously angry, once she realized, oh just *blazing!* She rushed up to me in the pinacoteca and began screaming the most— She called me a— She c-called me—" and began to weep.

(Called her what? I ran through my La Scala vocabulary. Empia? Infame? Sfrontata? Sciagurata? TRA-DI-TRI-CE?)

"Then I didn't see her for oh *days!*" she choked. "Oh I was in such dread such fear for her, and that minchione of a husband kept coming round moaning and bleating hadn't we heard from her? because she'd just *vanished*, Professor Shipley, and not even a word to me, as if she and I had never—I mean by that last morning I— Well actually I was in the kitchen peeling garlic, I was making an agliata and Hugh was in the salotto writing up his journal the way he'd started doing, *rearranging* what happened, half the time, and suddenly I heard this—suddenly Francesca— Oh, it happened!" she softly wailed; and her tears, this time, were for Hugh.

Francesca had it seems burst into the salotto absolutely raging—a cold foaming fountain of barely articulated Tuscan. Hugh must have got to his feet in courtliest astonishment, and the crazy girl pulled a little black pistol from her bag and shot him five times point-blank, the first three straight into his breast: he toppled back onto the writing table, gone already. Persis rushed in, wild with foreboding and disbelief, just in time to see his body slither like a heavy snake to the floor and hit flailing, and the sightless head thud and roll; and then it all eased, and lay still.

She pitched to her knees beside him, clutching at him, crying out, "But I love you *I love you!*" (the mindless, the beseeching magic of that incantation!)—and in helpless dismay found her fingers crimson with his blood. The plump little twin maids from across the landing raced in and at once began screeching. This brought their marchesa, who after one shocked glance cried, "But in the name of Our Lady of Heaven can't you run for a doctor?" at the now white and dully staring Francesca. Meekly beginning to weep, Francesca went. The old lady whipped an apron from a maid to staunch the weakening hiccups of blood; the maids fell to their knees crossing themselves and gabbled terrified prayers at Eternity. These various apotropaic measures were, of course, far too late.

All of which made a most rewarding news feature, the *Cor-*

riere della Sera stringer having arrived with the doctor and the police.

—And eventually I brought Hugh's body home. But the sepulchral and the fiscal bureaucracies that can embalm the Mediterranean dead, the winding-sheets of red tape, would, as they say in Rome, make Iddio's hair stand on end if He were bald. And Hugh was not just a corpse: he was a rather illustrious corpse. It was even maintained that, morally speaking, he was a cultural possession—classified, unexportable, in fact an Italian monument. So the patenti, the ricevute, the stylized and ritual disputes in this, that, and the other ministero or esattoria were as good as endless.

Not to mention the question of his—Il signore ci scuserà, ma Signore Tatnall's . . . to say "houseguest"? (Ahhh what a man of taste, l'illustre defunto!—what year after year after *year* always new beautifuls!) But exactly what, Signore Scippli, was this one's condizione civile? A man of the world like il signore testamentary executor had hardly to be reminded that in these cases one gravely risks—if il signore knew the term?—*mal-ver-sa-zi-o-ne*: "Sir, they *make off* with things!" By the time I got Hugh landed dockside in Boston I was in a state of exasperation that stopped just short of scrawling *Corpse—no value* on the customs declaration.

—And now (I thought drowsily) in how few hours more, the heavy dust I had had my lifelong friend reduced to was to be put into the earth at last, a few formal sad final words spoken over it as epicedium, and then—ah, Hugh, goodbye.

Except that here—history being we are told a series of logical consequences—here I now found myself with *this* particular benison of girl, and never mind the ghosts.

And dozed unregretfully off.

—Though somewhere in the night she woke me, to murmur, ". . . you're still *there?* sweetie what fidelity," tucking her bottom affectionately into my midriff.

Adding, all sleepy softnesses again, ". . . like two spoons."
And back to dream.

I I

The charm of such phrases ought not, I need hardly say, to
have lingered on, indulging my memory with their blandishments, as we sat side by side in the pious hush of the meetinghouse late the next morning.

I was, after all, brought up a Quaker. Loosely and non-
observantly, yes. But at least taught the ordinary godless decencies of Hicksite good manners.

Even reminded, if now and then my parents thought of it,
that Meeting is a time when thy mind is to be engaged with
Befitting Things—including whatever happens to be thy notion of God, even if peculiar.

At any event *not* anything as theologically out of place as
thinking about the pleasure of Camilla with pleasure.

For, simply, she happened to be beside me there, eyes cast
down as in angel meditation, gloved hands clasping what
looked like an Episcopal prayerbook, at a memorial service for a
years-past lover. And I was merely the escort who had, as is
proper, fetched her.

Just as I had fetched Persis too, here on my blameless other
side, a very sleek young widow indeed, in black even to the
faceted glitter of jet at the lobe of that charming ear, the pale
gold of her hair drawn flashingly back and up into a classic
knot.

Nevertheless, it was Hugh's mortal part that was to be
commemorated here, not his fine taste in young women. I had
fetched them both for sober Quaker purposes. Nothing more.

(And besides: If I were to glance at Camilla, and she by
simultaneous chance at me, it might well turn out not to be

Hugh our eyes would say to each other we were remembering.)

So we sat, the place now rapidly filling.

—My Arts-faculty colleagues were turning up en masse. Not that they approved of Hugh: many of them even thought him an outrage. But he had been artist-in-residence at Smith, off and on, for the better part of two decades—at any rate often there at least part of a semester, and the college had in principle the cachet of his presence even when he was somewhere else. Scandalized or not, our colleagues were having the piety, or at least the good manners, to acknowledge it.

A Quaker meetinghouse, if it is as old as it should be, has a vestigial partition down its center, each half with its own wide old entrance door from the street. A century and a half ago, one side was for women, one for men, and no glancing across: thee can just possess thy soul in patience till after Meeting. This meetinghouse had had its partition removed generations ago, but the ranks of long rail-backed deal benches stood where they had always stood, and marked the immemorial line. The tall old galleried room was dim in spite of the brilliance of early-summer noon outside, and full now of a kind of intense hush: silent and unstirring, eyes cast soberly down, the still host of Hugh's colleagues and mourners were settling into the sculptured attitudes of contemplation.

What I myself was contemplating, as the tedious minutes began to drone along, was not man's dutiful expectation of Eternity, as was solemn and approved, nor even Hugh's random prospects of it, or my own. Simply I began to think how long I had known him. How long and, I suppose, how well. And not just the fiery drive and arrogance of his painting, or his happy rampage after this or that fluttering girl—not even whether the painter and the libertine were two aspects or components of a creative unity—but merely the warm social animal he was with me instead, seen now through the haze of time.

For Hugh Tatnall had been my friend and second self from prep school and Princeton on. Arcades ambo, though the benchmarks of our spiritual topographies were altogether unlike. I come of well-to-do Chester County Quaker mill-owners; but Hugh was so impeccably upper-class Philadelphia that only the accident of an exotic upbringing can have saved him from being that and not much else. For until he was twelve he was raised, his parents having died young, by a rich expatriate uncle, an amiable rake who had a palazzo in Rome as well as the one in Florence, a castelletto in Portofino, an eighteenth-century view of life, and in particular a succession of titled mistresses, English and Italian, who fussed indulgently over little Hugh in flattery of his uncle, and in effect formed his young mind. As Hugh once said to me, "By god I was *ten* before it occurred to me that he might ever have gone to bed with a girl who wasn't at least a viscountess. . . ."

The consequence of this elegant misinformation was not however the snobbery one might expect. Rather, the company of his uncle's poppets made him precociously humane. Their beauty and bel canto blandishments, their stylized good manners, the idle affections of the whole ambience, combined to give him a kind of Renaissance page's enlightenment. He grew up in the caress of transience. For these were love affairs, they were fleeting, no matter what passion or what fantasy had been their occasion, and Hugh's uncle was always therefore still enchantedly paying court, the girl always still indulged to her exulting heart's content—"the air was full of angels," Hugh put it once, and on every side was the half-incredulous delight one has in a new love. Even if, sometimes, when a sweet creature left, there were tears, this too was a lesson in the humane. And finally (and very practically) Hugh had as a model a man who believed that a woman in love is the luxury of luxuries, and behaved so, and was therefore rewarded in kind.

The sense of social maneuver that this developed in Hugh

was of course too suave for the scruffy Philadelphia prep-school life his uncle eventually shipped him back to. But it paid off even there: at one time Hugh had a string of dazzled Main Line little girls each of whom tenderly fed him fudge on her weekly afternoon. ("Weekends," he used to say in a voice of kindly amusement, "they have off.")

It was Italy, also, that turned him into a painter. The furniture of his uncle's palazzi included art in Italian profusion, and Hugh's first canvas was a try at copying a lush Roman copy of "an anonymous Tiepolo." At prep school he drew Palladian ruins, a form of homesickness that did wonders for his draftsmanship. By our last year at Penn Charter, though, he was drawing "girls as architecture" as well as Renaissance landscape: he did that virtuoso *Still Life with Cousin Georgiana's Bosom* (now at Cooper Union—discreetly retitled) the spring we graduated, to commemorate a rather breathless family seduction.

He had begun to be a virtuoso at that too by then—and mind you, in those days the spiritual logistics of talking even a very dazzled girl into bed with you could be daunting. I can't think of anyone of Hugh's level of competence then, in fact, except Buck (Decimus) St. Ledger, a Virginian classmate of ours that autumn at Princeton, and Buck was merely Apollonianly good-looking besides. "A lazy bastard who just happens to be catnip," Hugh used to complain. "Goddammit Shipley here are you and I manfully screwing our way up out of adolescence, doing our Darwinian damnedest, and all this indolent snake St. Ledger ever has to do— Doesn't he my god take any pleasure in the *craftsmanship* of the thing? What kind of mannerless behavior to a girl's finer feelings is that?"

This talent of Hugh's, however, by our junior year was developing into an assurance, not to say a heartlessness, that I now and then found disturbed me. I come from a quieter persuasion of Quakers than Hugh's sometimes worldly Philadelphians. I was of course brought up, like any "birthright

Friend," without any nonsense about not doing pretty much as I pleased. My parents had the sophistications of what would now be called an existentialist tradition, my mother's father having even been "read out of Meeting" for marrying a girl he'd decided to without bothering about the Meeting's permission first. (They soon took him back, and my new grandmother with him—after all, he owned the bank as well as the paper mills.) But existential or not, I was still given fairly clear notions of "what thee does and does not do" from the time I'd been taught to pay attention to what was said to me, and the criterion, if not the canon, usually turned out to be less what was or wasn't "moral" than simply what was kind or unkind. These are hardly college-age adjectives. But Hugh's marauding had I thought become something that girls of that decently behaved era had nothing even near the tactical apprenticeship to cope with. Dionysiac charm is all very well, and the flower-crowned rites of spring are our cultural heritage; but Hugh's persuasions to delinquency struck me as offhand to the point of self-complacency, and in fact his campus reputation (undergraduate scuttlebutt being what it is) took on the imperishable vitality of myth—as late as our thirtieth reunion I found myself still having to tell a classmate that that famous seduction of the daughters of a professor of animal psychology was *Casanova*'s, dammit, not Hugh's.

Still, I have to say, in extenuation, that there were girls even then, possibly plenty of them, who were now and then up to him. I remember, spring of junior year, overhearing a set of his preliminaries with one of them, a velvety Southern-belle type named Lucinda. It was the last club party before finals, and I had gone outside for a drink. The club kept its weekend applejack in the ivy outside a dining-room window, and I was just reaching for the jug when Hugh's voice came through the open window above me, murmuring something I couldn't distinguish, and then a girl's voice, tense.

"But where will you—would you be?"

"Edge of the golf course back of the Inn."

"What if I can't get away from him?"

"You *helpless?*"

Silence. I could almost feel the electricity. And mind you, he'd hardly met the girl till before dinner! He said something else too low to make out, and she said, "But when he's jealous *already?*"

Again I couldn't hear what he answered—probably something disingenuous: what had they done to be jealous *about*, for God's sake. But then I heard her voice, secret and soft, taunting, "If *I* can almost taste you, silly, don't you suppose he's noticed? . . ." and as I disentangled the jug from the ivy they drifted out of hearing.

And so help me, it wasn't two hours till he picked her up behind the Inn and drove her off for the rest of the weekend to a stud farm of his grandfather's across the Delaware in Bucks County.

I was stunned when he told me. I said, "But for God's sweet sake, Tatnall, *no chaperone?*"

". . . Farm manager's wife was there."

"In the house with you?"

"Wouldn't bed-check if she had been."

"But didn't she do the rooms?"

"What if she did?"

"What's this what-if-she-did? dammit, the sheets—"

"For God's sake who *sleeps* together?"

That part of the carnal logistics hadn't occurred to me. My innocence abashed me; I switched to an aspect I knew about. "But what in hell'd you and this Lucinda *do* all day between nights?"

"Sat around."

"Charming each other, huh."

"Charmed *me!*"

"Just sitting around, for God's sake?"

"Rode some too."

"Where'd she get a habit?"

"Trunk in the tack room."

"Ride well?"

"Hunts at home."

"Just rode and sat around, huh."

"Huh."

"Didn't get her to pose for you or anything?"

". . . Sort of."

"Sort of what? Shirt off? Pretty bosom and all?"

". . . Made a fuss."

"You're losing your grip," I said, "and a good thing for American womanhood," but who knows what did happen? My guess has always been that Lucinda is the (shirtless) girl in that lighthearted Picasso parody in Boston, *Lady Looking Minotaur Straight in the Eye*, though the face is too Picasso'd to be sure about.

(Except which of several ways a girl can look you straight in the eye *is* she looking you straight in the eye?)

—She may of course have had explanations at home, and they may not have been convincing. Hugh I remember received a postcard with nothing but !!!!!!! on it, went haring off to Richmond to find out what she meant by it, was ordered violently out of the house by her father, in an atmosphere crackling with metaphorical horse-whips, and I'm not sure ever saw her again. Certainly he spent an unruffled summer painting Mediterranean light at his uncle's castelletto in Portofino.

—Well, as Auden said about something else, Come, peregrine nymphs, delight your shepherds. But by our senior year, luckily, they'd begun to humanize (and re-educate) Hugh as well. This can be disconcerting: I've always suspected Hugh wasn't far from thunderstruck the early-winter weekend when, of all people, the serene young second wife of his departmental adviser decided she would acquire him.

When honest to god all he'd done was go round to pay a
duty call on the guy!

Merely *happened* he was at a conference in Utah!

Or one of those places. So he'd stayed for tea anyhow. She
was a lot younger than her husband. Also it developed she did
avant-garde reviews for the *Dial*. So he'd stayed for dinner
too.

Then after dinner they'd sat by the fire and, well, she'd read
Marianne Moore and stuff to him.

So, in brief, goddammit, and as good as straight out of
Dante, *Marianna fu il libro e chi lo scrisse*, hard as that is to
credit—

I said but for God's—

Was I going to tell him a mere Princeton senior was expected to argue with a *Dial* critic in *bed?* And dammit what
was I laughing at?—she was *wonderful!* And also, for all he
knew he might have got her in a hell of a jam: it had *snowed*
in the night (of all possible acts of God to have occurred!),
and there in the new snow were his footprints only coming
out—with every faculty neighbor in Broadmead sure as hell to
know exactly when the stuff had started falling *and* when it
had stopped!

—Drawing-room farce, yes. And it didn't have a long run:
second term her husband disobligingly took her off with him
on a sabbatical. But it was Hugh's first affair with a girl just
enough sensual and civilizing years older to put an end to his
adolescence; and the face with a look of hers that turned up in
Hugh's canvases for several years afterwards is less I think a
symbol or a memory than payment of a debt.

Senior year, too, he had his first one-man show. It was only
local, at the Brick Row Book Shop, and in the main just Mediterranean landscape and Italian hill towns—what a petulant
critic later described as "Mr. Tatnall's revolting cold-color
lotissements." But two of these same early canvases brought

solid prices three years ago at Sotheby's, and even Princeton undergraduates got a sense of what an astonishing young painter he was: in our senior balloting he was even voted *both* "Most brilliant" and "Thinks he is," the second as solid a mark of status as the first.

—So in due course we graduated. More or less cum laude, even doing very little work. Though why work if one has natural prerogatives? Who in Art-and-Architecture could even begin to draw like Hugh? Nor did I think anybody in Classics could, say, turn out neater Latin elegiacs than I did. I was especially fond of an Ovidian farewell to a two months' Vassar love of mine. I can still remember how it began:

> Tamquam nocte brevi longum ponamus amorem:
>   Voce unâ partam perdat et una fidem—

which I translated for her

> Put off our long, like a brief evening's, love:
> The bond one word began, let one word end.

So cum laude and a credit to our various departments we graduated, and went our several ways.

—And between that lighthearted airy morning long ago and this one now (I thought, contemplating the hushed and reverent assemblage of Hugh's colleagues on every side about me, row on unstirring row)—between then and now think what rectitudes his life and conduct, by contrast, had comfortingly allowed them to display. What fastidiously intellectual deprecations he had been the occasion of, what campus head-shakings, what disparagements, how many high-minded and improving senses of outrage, what universal chiding! All moreover how justified and unanswerable: for paint, yes, certainly—but why not lead a respectable life *too*? . . .

The meeting house door creaked open and closed again one

last time, the old flat latch clacked, a final late-come friend bustled breathily to some bench behind us and settled with deprecatory scufflings. Silence took over. By some unspoken consensus it came to be understood that the formal hour had begun. The door held its peace, the latch was mute, the last apologetic rustlings died away, and in grave and quiet meditation Meeting began.

I I I

Quaker funerals have no prescriptive ritual. The *Book of Discipline* says merely, "We commend the simplicity of our usual form of worship" and lets it go at that. But our usual form of worship happens to be formless: one just sits, in a meeting-house, in silence, for one hour. Thee may of course get to thy feet and speak if thee is moved to. And, in principle, on any topic. Even if peculiar.

But, in Hugh's case, what to say? Recite the standard graveside pieties one could not, Hugh being Hugh: *this* undeceived forgathering knew better. And whatever went on here ought in any case, it had seemed to me, to be for *his* ghostly entertainment, not the Smith faculty's—their taste in iusta funebria was irrelevant.

Also, who was to say whatever was to be said? Plausible numberers of the usual nonsense wouldn't do. Nor would any speaker who didn't know exactly what he was getting into. I had finally drafted a man who was pretty much a fellow-marauder of Hugh's, an engaging Carolinian named (to give him his full Rebel quarterings) Taige Pulteney Massingberd Heald, a years-long friend, colleague, and campus libertine whose charm was as breathless a student legend as Hugh's own.

I did have some trouble talking him into it (why pick on *him* for my spiritual requirements?). But I'd said now now, think how a fellow-campaigner's words of appreciation would please Hugh's ghost as it passed upward to higher preoccupations. And with a consoling reassurance that it was leaving the student body in such good hands still. So there at any rate he now sat, "facing the Meeting" as it's called, looking put-upon and wary.

The slow, sobering, pointless minutes began to drowse their lengths along. A throat was self-effacingly cleared; somebody sighed deeply. Camilla lifted a black-gloved thumb and finger and delicately adjusted an earring. Persis humbly swallowed a tiny yawn. Up at the front, Taige recrossed his well-tailored knees and settled on the other buttock; his disinclinations began to show. And on every side, in stony tedium, row on row, aligned like sepulchral statues along an ancient Roman way, the silent synod of Hugh's assizers and assoilers began resolutely sitting out the hour.

—But what could any such alliterated establishment ever have made of Hugh, I said to myself, bisected or not into those indispensable academic entities (a) the Man and (b) the Œuvre. His canvases with their maelstroms of fractured and re-constituted light are in museums and millionnaires' collections everywhere. Yet here, three rows ahead of me in this intellectual assemblage, sat our famous old physiologist who at a campus show of Hugh's had been overheard remarking, with mild asperity, "Why, bless me, the human genitalia don't look like that!" ("Have I painted a girl then or a goddam dahlia?" Hugh snorted.) But Hugh's renown in the college had never been quite clear: as in other disciplines too, the Work was always being somehow confused with the Man. One sarcastic and slighting colleague had even declared, "The fellow's major work's his endless damn' girls anyhow!" And a Lesbian wit had nicknamed one of his portraits "Tatnall's lunch."

College girls' falling in love with faculty, as any reasonably masculine professor knows, was a rite of academic anthropology many long years before anything as simpleminded as sexual freedom was thought up. The explanation of those days was of course Freudian, a happy search for someone like Father in age and authority—and what's a professor if not an authority? and, well, *sort* of old! And, well, with a professor, voilà, it isn't incest.

(Though think how much Hegelized nonsense Freud might have left unwritten if he'd just been what we used to call *around* a little. Or had even come across that urbane sentence of Steele's: "She naturally thinks, if she is tall enough, she is wise enough for anything for which her education makes her think she is designed.")

The quantification of such an agreeable perquisite did at one time make private-college administrations jumpy. "Though Simon goddammy," Hugh would complain, "am I to tell some trusting child she *doesn't* love me? Frustrating her temporary view of what she's here on earth for? If a campusful of girls feel they have to fall in love, what business have our trustees behaving as if they thought this decorous young ladies' seminary was an upper-class house of call?"

But, generally no doubt, why or how Hugh painted was beyond his average colleague's grasp. Whereas often I knew even the trivial detail. That madonna series, for instance: if future art scholars bother with it, they will naturally spot the parody of the Raphael series in which the Virgin holds the bambino in the curve of one arm, and, in the other hand, some symbol of the crucifixion to come. But how are they to guess that Hugh's series began as a private joke?

One of his first girls at Smith was, it happened, a very pretty but also a very proper Mormon. Her name was Susannah; and though she seems to have had only sporadic religious crises about making love with Hugh, once she got used to it, he never could get the child to pose for him. She was terribly sweet and humble about this, but she absolutely would not. A chaste head and shoulders, yes, but oh please please nothing more.

"And was *I* to put up with that kind of disingenuous farce?" he demanded of me. "So I *painted* her as a virgin by god! That book in her hand's the Book of Mormon to prove it. The bambino's chubby little hand that's just pulled her shirt off's a work of the imagination too."

But when he let his model see it, her shock of dismay at the composition was shattering. She gave a little cry of woe and stared at it speechless, and when at last she turned to Hugh her face was sheer hopeless misery.

Now now *now*, he'd said, why, what on earth was this?—had she forgot her art history altogether? Did he need to remind as good a student as she was that, say, Fouquet had painted Agnès Sorel as the Virgin? *And* with that charming left bosom of hers as bare as in her secular portraits? Was she a fine-arts major or wasn't she?

She looked at him with great wet eyes, wordlessly betrayed.

"So, like a perfect gent," he said to me in his humanest tone, "I simply handed the child a palette knife and said all right, all right, it's yours anyway, my angel, slash the wicked thing to ribbons."

I said but naturally she hadn't?

"When *I*'d painted her portrait?" he cried, affronted.

Or again, what historian can guess the cockeyed history of the 'Bona Dea Motif' of later canvases in the series, that veiled female figure one faintly makes out lurking half-hidden in the edge of a shadowy Tuscan-hillside wood in so many of the backgrounds.

The Bona Dea is an obscure Latin vegetation spirit who became, as times grew less primitive, an anthropomorphic goddess of love; but for some reason Hugh had taken her as his tutela. I'm not sure he didn't half-believe it *was* She Who gave him (or sometimes, for Her own amusement, denied him) whatever girl he had at the moment an eye on. This nonsense had derived from a casual affair at Nîmes, years before. A ship's stewardess, a pretty Nîmoise, had obligingly sewn a button on a shirt for him, and while she sewed they had talked; and later talked several times more; and a few weeks later, en route from Nice to Biarritz, he seems to have thought why not stop off and see.

His train had pulled into Nîmes during a violent thunderstorm. At the very moment he stepped off, there was a frightful rending crash, the platform shook, women travelers shrieked and swooned, and simultaneously (he presently discovered) the Maison Carrée was struck by lightning. This, in a landscape of ancient pagan gods like Provence, was a clear Omen.

And of what, he soon found out. The girl not only sighed into his arms without a moment's demurring, she spent the rest of her vacation there, except when she was posing for him, or cooking for him, or washing his clothes.

This struck him as a demonstration of Who was In Charge of him (and with thunderbolts at Her disposal!); and when presently he wandered through the public gardens looking for the Maison Carrée but somehow failed to find it, that was part of the monstrum too: the Bona Dea had caused it to vanish, to remind him. "Elle exagère, ta déesse," said the girl.

(Whom he immortalized as befits such an epiphany. She is that glowing *Girl with Two Shirts* in the art museum at Princeton, perched on the windowsill of her kitchen in the flooding pagan brilliance of Mediterranean noon, legs dangling bare; she has just sewn a button on a yellow shirt and is biting off the thread; the other shirt, unbuttoned, is what she more or less has on. Picked out in black tiles on the red-tiled floor, as if an ancient Roman had put his admonitory CAVE CANEM there, you can just make out a DÉESSE MÉCHANTE.)

—On the far side of the meetinghouse a towering old man I had never seen before in my life abruptly stood up, and in a strong gobbling voice ejected a couple of stanzas of what I took to be, from their tone of meek piety and general theological smarm, some Quaker poet or other. He then sat down as sud-

denly as he had got up, and the silence of empty-headed meditation engulfed us once more.

Persis looked at me with great startled lovely eyes. Camilla
made a faintly mocking face, lips shaping a soundless *Who?*

I soundlessly mouthed back *Gonnd*.

I   V

And we'll get more of it from the same exhortatory Source, I
said to myself, delight in the repetition of claptrap being what
it is, if Taige doesn't get *on* with whatever his prepared damn'
remarks about Hugh turn out to be.

—Though what was I to conclude Hugh "was," here at the
melancholy end of it? What had the guesses of history ever
made of, say, Benvenuto Cellini? How explain any of these
sporadic fusions of creative genius and incurable libertine that
decorate the record of our cultural heritage? What made that
wild meteor of the Restoration, Lord Rochester, go in for so
much sheer outrage—how explain Liszt, or Byron? Half the
girls in their endless baggage-trains seem to have as good as
mistaken them for reincarnations of the primordial Dionysus,
and themselves as initiates in their thiasoi.

> If history points a moral (and we *say* it does)
>   Don Juans are immortal—that wild spirit
> That makes the female heart behave the way it does
>   The moment a marauding male comes near it.

("And often to its fluttering own dismay it does," one can
add, cooings of palumbiform goddesses or not.)

But certainly, in Hugh's case, the expatriate uncle's example, if not his influence, had somehow to have molded him. I
remember his telling me of a long-ago morning when, as a
very small boy, he was pattering about the terraced gardens of

his uncle's castelletto in Portofino, and first saw, dazzled, what was probably the loveliest, and certainly the most scandalous, of his uncle's beltà, Lady Mary Castinge: that instant could have formed the pattern.

Lady Mary (this generation has to be told) was one of *the* international beauties of her day. The *Tatlers* and *Spectators* and *Sketches* of the twenties are one long photographers' tribute to her angelic English loveliness, and to the Almanach de Gotha of her misbehaviors. She was born (see Debrett) Lady Mary Sare; but by the customary processes of British upper-class marriage, adultery, divorce, remarriage, and nomenclature, she successively became Lady Mary Savenake-Hope, Lady Mary de Wennerent, Lady Charles Penhér, and finally, married to Capt. the Hon. Philip Castinge, became Lady Mary again. That time at Portofino, if I have the chronology right, she was being divorced to become Lady Charles. Or was Penhér the fellow who was divorcing her? Not that it matters, or mattered then. She used to come floating devotedly back to Hugh's uncle between husbands anyhow. "*Much* her favorite co-respondent," Hugh said.

But to five-year-old Hugh, trotting busily about the climbing gardens that innocent morning, when he looked up and saw her coming languidly up the flights of broad stone steps on his uncle's arm, white and gold in that clarity of Ligurian light, she was divinity. He had had a mildly mythological bringing-up: we were all read to at bedtime then from a genteel scarlet-bound expurgation of cultural anthropology called *The Children's Hour*, so he knew what gods and goddesses were. But the draftsmanship of *The Children's Hour* illustrations was on the muddy side: what goddesses, in particular, looked like was hard to make out. Now he *saw*: they looked like This Lady.

She was saying in one of those cool rippling English voices "—but you can't think Robert what a doting wife I should have made you darling, who else do I indulge with this spouse-like and wedded constancy, you will admit? Eccomi, after every marriage! Or should one rebuke your vanity and say 'before'?" (Or this is what Hugh thought she said. To a small boy it was meaningless. Also, the fluting English of her accent made him uncertain whether she was speaking a language he knew.) "*Ohhh* how you look at me, you look as if all you can think of when you see me is the wicked things you persuade me to do with you, goodness isn't it heaven! But now Robert who's *this*, you're not to tell me he's some son of yours darling, I suppose his mother's some sweet farrowing little Italian piece you've had somewhere?"

Hugh's uncle said firmly no, no: nephew, nephew. Right side of the blanket too, far as *he* knew; and Hugh come here be presented.

But she was saying, "Now Robert *how* implausible, he's the most melting image of you!"

(So he *was* understanding what she said—this remark he had heard before. That girl who'd spent part of the spring with them, and left in a fiery tantrum of tears only a few days before, had once in his hearing told his uncle the same thing: "Ma fa paura, carino, quanto ha il tuo aspetto. . . .")

His uncle said oh nonsense, resemblance didn't make the boy a by-blow—*he* didn't indulge in the coarse practices of the peerage and landed gentry! and she said yes he *was* always maintaining he was a landed peasant instead, wasn't he, what a staring snob he was! and laughing affectionately in each other's faces they went lazily on up into the castelletto beyond.

All little Hugh could do was gaze and gaze, his senses drowning in her radiance. He gave up breathing entirely. He was not merely transfigured with awe, he was stunned with love. "In fact," he once told me, "I forgot that adorable contessa of Uncle Robert's on the spot—a girl who'd been tenderly mothering me for weeks, girl who'd leave my uncle and race to my room at two in the morning if I had a nightmare, and snatch me up in her warm young arms and croon comforting Italian to me and carry me back to her own bed with her. I even remember my uncle standing there once at the foot of her bed, in a pool of moonlight, laughing 'Dunque!—sono cornuto anch'io!' There I'd been, five years old in bed by god with my first girl—and I forgot her *instantly*, for that cool and heavenly being on Uncle Robert's arm. What perfidy! What benefits forgot!"

—Though, again, how much of Hugh's behavior at Smith was due, rather, to the delectable environment, that always changing campus population of girls he had lived among off and on for so long? There they were—self-willed, flighty, ungovernably amorous, dithery, lawless, innocent, ruthlessly designing, demure, sly. Ma ahimè, incantevoli too; and how they threw themselves in his way! Having an affair with Hugh Tatnall, I've heard it sardonically argued, had become practically a status symbol. "Who sees goatishness as goatishness at nineteen?" Hugh used to argue. "Why, dammy, they still think it may be the Great God Pan."

(The fact, more likely, is that they used him and knew they did, and also more or less knew why. Whether he was an advanced lab course or the higher theory of the thing no doubt depended on a girl's previous disillusionments. But there he was, an undeniable paradigm of what a lover was supposed to be; and if in due course he too disillusioned them, it was disillusion as good as certified on a higher level entirely.)

Faculty wives were sometimes affected too. He had hardly settled in, I remember, his first year at Smith, before the young wife of an instructor in French (a Structuralist, come to think of it—compounding the nonsense!) took to "confiding" in him. Did he think, she would ask him mournfully, that everybody worked as *tirelessly* at their dissertations as her husband? Did they all spend so much *time* at the college—evenings too? Did he think some horrid sneaky girl— She wept, flowerlike and enravishing, against Hugh's breast pocket; had to be comforted, brow kissed and so forth; soon, too, those great tear-filled and doleful eyes. Lovely grieving curve of her neck too, below her little jeweled ear. And so, ah well, around, at last, to lips still wet and tremulous with her tears. This is all so childish that I am embarrassed to remember it of a friend.

Yet all Hugh had to say was what was I snorting at! Had I forgot Benjamin Constant's pointed phrase about "le despotisme de leur douleur"? Was it *his* fault if some over-articulate sod in Modern Languages hadn't structured his wife's reading in the Romantics? And anyhow, dammit,

> Elles nous font autant
> De pluies que de beaux temps

for our own good, don't they? To keep our sensibilities in working order, at no matter what cost to their own? Was he *not* to assuage such high-minded tears? Was I a stone? ...

—Well, as Lord Byron wrote to Lady Melbourne, of Lady Frances Webster's oaf of a husband, "If a man is not contented with a pretty woman, he must not be surprised if others admire that which he knows not how to value." Anthropologists tell us that stealing women is only exogamy anyhow.

V

A soft sound from Camilla: Taige had got to his feet and was stepping gravely down into the broad aisle across the front of the meetinghouse.

Where he now stood for a silent moment contemplating us—bland, courtly, archaic-looking, and easy, as if this were a graduate seminar and his subject Aristotle's Ethics rather than Hugh's. But in fact it was in lay-sermon tones that he began:

"We are a people, I suggest to you, of the here and now."

A practiced Ciceronian pause. He'd decided to bore us high-minded? And talk *around* the factual Hugh; very ingenious.

He went on: "The theme of death as a long rest is as alien to us as it is Asiatic—the hopelessness of the slave mines of antiquity, Platonized into a contempt for life, and then, by lesser Platos, into a distaste for it."

I was amused. Not four hours earlier the disingenuous bastard had interrupted my breakfast at Camilla's to fuss about what under the sun he could say—he was doing my spiritual dirty work for me wasn't he? so then how about a few paragraphs of classical throwaways dammit from *me!*

—I had woken alone.

. . . Heartlessly deserted?

But no: off in the studio her grand piano was showering the summer morning with Baroque cadenzas. Not deserted—sweetly let sleep. The glittering notes fled in like handfuls of spilled jewels. Rehearsing for her next concert. So no "eyelids lifting upon a matutinal Pygmalion." Just Mozart.

And breakfast fed me by her willowy au pair sophomore, leering as if sophisticated. I was still feeding when in sauntered Taige.

"Not having found you at home," he explained in courteous unsurprise. He pulled a chair to the table and stared round at the food. So I'd taken to acquiring musical culture too, had I?—though would I *listen* to what that unfeeling girl was playing? And on the very day of her once-cherished Hugh's funeral!

I said come come. And to have some coffee.

"Ah but Simon *this* sonata!" he cried. "Have you any notion how it brings back my own charming little—bless my soul what was her name? Had a silly affair with Hugh before I got her."

He meant Emma?

"That's it—*Emma.* Dear heaven Simon what a fantasia of a girl! Past poor Hugh's ability to appreciate I suspect altogether. D'you know, she'd say, 'Oh my darling when you weep for me what do you weep for me *to?*' What's a man to say?—

so at random I told her to *this* adagio: good as anything else. It became our 'theme.' Bless your heart, I *must* have told you."

I said he had, yes.

"But does it I wonder still move me now, though," he said, as if judicially, listening. "What if I found myself fearing it no longer does, Simon. Have I a heart of granite, would you say? Or less sensibility than I hope my sensibilities deserve? Ah, well. Yes. Emma. She'd say, '*Oh* how I love you temporarily!' Isn't that charming? Isn't that witty? All what long years now past and gone. Why do any of us. Yes. Well. Happiness, how sad. And now we've got to put dear old fornicating Hugh's dust in the grave too. We shall miss the turmoil of his depredations."

Though now what about this oration he'd had the madness to say he'd undertake for me. Would I tell him what he could possibly say with a straight face? "Hugh's undeviating interest in the individual student." Ho ho ho. "The enviable campus reputation of the Tatnall seminar." *Ho* ho ho. As they sat there tutting their moral tuts. Had I forgotten what faculty meetings were like?

—A sunburst of crashing final chords from the studio, then silence; and then in a moment there in the doorway had been Camilla, eyes as if veiled in the sonata's concluding intensities —barely even taking us in, lost still in the Mozart, in purest technician's trance. She drifted across to the table, a musing angel in work shirt and torero breeches, black curls pulled up into her concert chignon all anyhow, absently holding up a polite cheek to each of us in turn to be kissed—murmuring a still abstracted "Mmmmm *pet*" to Taige from her reverie, and a dreamy "*Mmmmm* sweetie" to me.

Then so to speak she saw me. And came mockingly awake. "You got *up?*—goodness!" she said, sat sweetly down in my chair, and rang for a fresh verseuse of coffee.

(O lovely dish from heaven that you are, I said to myself,

by what dazing Mediterranean inadvertence of Hugh's goddess was last night appointed and conferred on *me*? . . .)

She was saying to Taige, "But goodness what a great glum
fussing face, what *can* be wrong?" so the cynical anguishes of
his dilemma were still being re-explained when I finished my
breakfast and left to fetch Persis.

Camilla saw me off.

I said, "Kiss for the road?"

"Why?"

"I got *up!*"

"Such enterprise!"

I drove off laughing. But then I found myself thinking
about her with such happy violence that I pulled into the next
filling station and rang her up.

"Why, it's you," she said. "Where are you?"

"In a phone booth."

"A phone booth where?"

"It doesn't say."

"But what's wrong?"

"Nothing's wrong."

"I thought you were fetching the little widow."

"I am. I'm en route."

"Then *what*, sweetie?"

"You mean I don't make sense?"

A silence. Then, "Are you going to *say* why you're calling?"

"What I wasn't given a chance to, this morning."

Another silence, shorter. Then she said sweetly, "Was good
for your morale, last night?"

"What a question!"

"Well I should think so!"

"Was good for yours?"

"What vanity!"

We hung up, snickering, and I drove off.

It had been late, the night before. We had just finished

shutting up her house for the night, I the polite guest lending a hand; we were just leaving the studio. All evening we had discussed Hugh. Or perhaps I should put it, thematically we were discussing Hugh, and what ostensibly we were discussing was our relationships to him, but in simple fact what we were doing was exploring our relationship with each other now Hugh was gone. Memories we shared of him were also memories of our own unstated hankering earlier, and not stating it now was beside the point: every phrase of reminiscence had become a kind of subliminal serenade, hour after hour.

We left the studio; she flicked off the light at a switch by the door into the hall. And at that moment she turned to me in the darkened doorway and said, as if summing up the evening about Hugh and his girls, "And that was always the trouble, sweetie, he didn't always *like* us as we are."

So all I had to say was, "But you've decided maybe I do? . . ." and she said, "Well, you *do*," with suave approval, and stepped into my arms.

—What an angel what an angel. I pulled into another filling station like an infatuated boy and rang her number.

". . . You *again?*"

"I thought perhaps by this time Taige—"

"He hasn't."

"You mean he's *still* discuss—?"

"Sweetie are you calling for information or do you just love me?"

(What kind of lopsided disjunction was that? I was simple-mindedly out of my mind about her!)

I said, "The first time I ever saw you—"

"But you were just an old friend of his that he'd bored me going on about half the summer, at Portofino."

"Whereas *I*, with a certain adulterous gallantry—"

"Sweet Simon did I *stay* bored?"

Silence again; it was all elliptical anyhow. Our minds went wordlessly on. Until I said, "Are you smiling?"

"Yes."

"At bogus discussions?"

"You mean I discussed him with you and see what happened?"

"Angel *angel*," I said, "why did you get up?"

". . . That wasn't in your plans?"

" 'Plans'?—when I hadn't seen you for months?"

". . . Well what did you think then, before?"

"What seeing you again would be like."

"See, you did plan!"

"What did *you* think, before?"

"Oh . . . I wondered what you'd be like again, too. After all these months. Nearly a year. And I thought, well, here we'd *be*. In my empty house, all alone. Just the private two of us, in my dark empty house. Listening to the beating of our hearts. . . . Oh, just the customary maidenly thoughts, sweetie! And wondering whether—well, what *were* you like. . . ."

V I

I surfaced, sighing.

And found Taige in full gnomic cry: ". . . so that for the average man among us, hardly will even the syllables of his name outlive the fading recollections of those who knew him. In the ancient Attic idiom, élathe biôn—'he escaped notice living,' and this is the common lot. But for illustrious men, as Pericles said of the Athenian dead, a whole earth is a memorial, extinction in part suspended. . . ."

—And this was the panourgos who'd come badgering me for classical throwaways!

What's more, with a theme like extinction, it struck me Taige was running risks. Those flesh-hacking battlefields of 431 B.C. are on record and, now and then, remembered; but the lumbering hoplites cut down on them are not—Pericles's grandiose "a whole earth" is not an identifying stele. Yet who, out of Hugh's lifetime roster of infatuated girls, could Taige or anyone be sure had so much as bothered to read the news of his death? Or been saddened if they had. Or had come here this summer morning if only for a wordless moment of farewell. (Or for that matter, Camilla my angel, been one night faithful to a ghost before its nunc dimittis into oblivion.)

This, mind you, when girl after girl had imagined she was making over her life for him; and I thought of Caroline, an absolutely classic case of a love affair with a thoroughly nice girl.

Caroline was the fifth young wife (or perhaps the sixth: one lost count) of a majestic professor of English Lit named Coplestone Colville, a much-sought-after performing poet cum visiting lecturer, both here and abroad, who had made a practice of marrying his students. Caroline was almost thirty years younger than he and hadn't I believe gone to bed with him her senior year, but otherwise she was very much like her predecessors—demure, sensual, innocent, determined, and, as far as the Bona Dea sees fit, idealistic.

At the wedding, Hugh had been more sardonic about Cope than usual. "Are his damn' girls coming in primary colors now?" he grumbled to me. "*Look* at the Velásquez red of that delicious mouth. And the misty radiance of her eyes—Corot-blue by god if there ever was!"

I said why not borrow the girl?—he could do a *Virgin on the Dean's List* from her.

"Dean's List *was* she then?" he cried, delighted. "*That*'s what Cope thinks the List's for? . . ." And I doubt if he gave her another thought.

But that next summer, on Cape Cod, he'd rented a cottage in a part of Chatham known as Skunks Neck (he was working on the second version of his *Sea-Light Triptych*) and Caroline happened to be on the Cape too. And temporarily alone: Cope had gone magisterially off on a cultural tour of the Balkans for the State Department—*not* her sort of project, he'd explained to her: living conditions were primitive, the schedule was exhausting, he'd have to be what was called available-to-students fifteen hours a day, and there was no food worth eating east of Vienna anyway; so he had deposited her in a house somebody had lent him in Wellfleet. As a summer project, she was reading Virginia Woolf entire. This, in a young wife as beautiful as Caroline, is an inscrutable omen.

And Hugh, at a loose end somewhat too, found himself seeing to her social life. He sailed with her; he amiably lugged her hamper at picnics; he squired her to parties. He even got hold of a small racing sloop and had her as crew. She fed him lunch a couple of times a week in return. They discussed Virginia Woolf, the erotic sociology of the Eastern college girl, marine navigation, the father-daughter relationship, and (often) each other. Probably for ten days they were as blameless as Homer's blameless Ethiopians.

But then one night a Harwich Port millionnaire with intellectual leanings gave a party for a Cambridge don who was on a pilgrimage to Edmund Wilson. Wilson himself didn't come but socially it was a great success: everyone drank to the point of oratory. I myself, I find I remember, no longer conversed— I declaimed. My classicist's bred-in dismissal of English Lit was available to anybody who'd shut up and listen. I even remember charging out into the warm summer starlight, glass in hand, as Hugh was taking Caroline home, crying out where was *he* going, in God's name, with a girl who'd affronted our cultural heritage by marrying into *English?*—'d he mistaken *their* departmental taste for sexual selection God help us all? Caroline had had to kiss me half a dozen laughing good nights before I'd let them take off.

It was one of those black and brilliant early-summer nights, a dusky splendor of starlight over everything, the earth in inky shadow. And very late, the moon long set; the sleeping villages they drove through were dark and silent, the roads deserted, the distant beaches invisible, only now and then the ivory lines of surf glimmering faint and far off as they thrust their fans of foam up the unseen sand. But for a car's headlights once far away among the dunes, the towering night was like a great dim ballroom in which they found themselves alone. A more elegant setting for a seduction a girl couldn't reasonably have asked for. Or the Bona Dea provided.

At Caroline's gate, when he handed her out of his car, for a wordless moment she faced him, poised in the dark radiance of starlight like starlight herself in her floating summer dress— *She's like jewels* he told me he remembered thinking. Her beauty astonished him as if he were seeing it for the first time —and the dreaming gaze, the eyes lifted to him as Corot-blue no doubt he thought as ever but in the darkness what was their expression? a soft wonder, like the night about them? . . . Never mind what; he reached out and took her in his arms.

And was instantly incredulous. Like a telegraph of doom, his libertine synapses flashed it to him almost before their delight: this delicious girl was not just in his arms but, beyond any ambiguity, was *his!*—even this lovely mouth had never kissed anyone with *this* abandon. He was scandalized. And from the periphery what corroborating data were flooding in —the warm weight of her, clinging, melting, handed over, title and tenure as good as conferred in fee simple forever.

And how past dissembling it was clear she knew it too when at last she fought loose, gasping and wild, hair tumbling, eyes dazed, lost—for, simply, everything had been said. They faced each other, and you could have said what they faced, like a starlight presence between them, was Cope. Then she broke free, with a choking little cry of dismay, and fled into the house.

He was more or less dumfounded. The light went on in her hall; then the light on the stair; then the light in the hall went out and in her bedroom a light went on. But at once went off again, and when it came on the curtains had been drawn. If he had not been so upset for her he would have laughed aloud. He got back into his car and drove back to Chatham, shaking his head at himself.

Though God *damn* Cope! This unguarded *angel* of a girl!—who now couldn't pretend even to herself that the difference between Cope and him wasn't open, explicit, calamitous, irreversible, and apparently heaven.

With every immemorial station and sequence of love now how inevitable!—meetings; tears; transports; protestations and accusations; flights. . . .

And he himself, routine or not, he too might easily by god find himself declaring—even believing: for how often had he not!—that this delectable state of things, this tender woe, a girl *in love* like this, might never if he did not take her come his way again. He pulled in at his cottage groaning with simplemindedness.

His telephone was ringing. He charged through the door.

It had stopped. He was *outraged*.

Though what could he have said, if he'd got to it in time, that any longer needed saying anyhow?

She of course in no time rang again. "Hugh?"

"Are you all right?" he cried.

Silence. Then she said, "I wanted—I just— You did get home all right? I just thought—"

The connection broke.

She immediately rang back. "Oh my darling I didn't mean to hang up!"

"Huh?"

"You— We didn't say good night."

Neither did she say it now. Or hang up. But said softly, "Will I see you tomorrow? When will I see you?"

"It's already tomorrow."

"Today then? This morning? *Soon?*"

"I was going to Boston."

"I know. You said. *Are* you going?"

"After *tonight?*" he said, in shocked gallantry.

She cried, "Well how could I be sure!" as if furious.

Silence again. He said, "*Are* you all right, Caro?"

"Will you *stop* asking me that *stupid* question!"

"I was only—"

"When you went away and *left* me like that!—when for all I knew I might never see you again, you could have been killed in an accident! And just when we'd— My darling, you *left* me! I thought of that Henry James girl who said 'If I knew how I felt I should die,' and I could have shrieked it aloud, so there!"

And hung up.

Hugh sat there. Dutifully feeling, I imagine, that he should feel stricken. The very phone in his hand denounced him: what had he done? Perhaps at that very moment she had begun to weep. *That* was what he had done!

Though what was civilization good god coming to?—modern girls *upset* at being upset about a man!

And look what he'd got anyway from meditating seduction in the English department: quotations from Henry James. . . .

So he went snickering amiably to bed.

—Tossed for a good while, though. For what, humanely, was he to make of her being overcome at herself to this degree? Or make of such a vaudeville of contradictions, both horns of the dilemma showing simultaneously. . . . It was the first pallors of summer dawn before he slept.

—A little cry of rage was what woke him. He opened his eyes; and there she stood, poised in his bedroom doorway, smoldering.

"You could *sleep?*" she cried at him, in a passion.

He was too stunned at how beautiful she was to know what she was talking about.

"*Asleep!*—what we've done doesn't mean anything more to you than that?" she upbraided him, tears of sheer affront in her eyes. "My darling love don't you even understand what's *happened?*"

He sat up, saying, "Caro—"

"And now you don't even care enough about my feelings to put a dressing-gown on!" she choked, and vanished from the doorway.

Well but dear god he at least had pajama trousers on!—so he sprang out of bed and plunged after her. She was just running out of the cottage. He yelled "But goddammit I *adore* you!" at her, and she stopped in her tracks and leaned against the doorjamb, weak and lovely, looking at him in wet-eyed misery, lips quivering.

Was she out of her *senses?* he cried. Did she think that any man, ever, had been blessed with a more—

"But we can't!" she wept (answering some other question). "Oh Hugh we *can't!*" in sheer woe dissolving into his arms. "Because *do* you love me—last night I thought you did, but do you?"—nonsense which he naturally answered by kissing her mournful mouth.

But she thrust him away. "Don't you understand what *has* happened, my darling?" she lamented. "This absolute heaven, of being in love like this, only then *not* free for it?"

He said what had a word like "free" have to do with the way a coup de foudre—

"Then oh *kiss me!*" she said violently; and this time, everything had been admitted in advance.

But as the logical sequence to what she was doing was what with anguish she had just assured him she could not do, presently she fell back against the doorjamb, disheveled and radiant, blissful, blue eyes dazed with deliverance. "*Ohhhh* the way you kiss me! oh if you ever got me into a bedroom and kissed me like that— Oh you *please* me so!" she babbled, mindless with happiness. The folly was complete: if he'd had any sense he'd have taken her then and there.

—The delirium of a new love is, normally, a kind of slow fever. But to Caroline it had happened instantaneously, in a thunderclap of shattered innocence, and she took off into the trecento like a cuor gentil born. She lost eight pounds in the first three days. She couldn't eat. She would wake at four in the morning and lie staring at the ceiling deep into the summer dawn. She began to have frightening dreams, often of an appalling clarity.

"You and I were standing in that arbor Cope has," she for example told Hugh, "but we didn't know each other somehow, not names or anything; my darling love we were just two figures in an arbor. I began telling you about a girl I knew who'd got amnesia. It was terribly sad, I said, because it had happened while she and her husband were making love, so of course there she was with *no idea* who this huge heaving man even was! It was *ignoble!* So you said to me, 'If that turned out to be you, you must or mustn't say so,' and I said, 'I ought never to know who you are again,' and I woke up *sobbing!*"

By the end of three days, between guilt and wild longing, she was half out of her mind in a kind of seething depression. She would say, in misery, "If I had any honor I wouldn't even listen to the lovely things you say to me, and if you had any honor you wouldn't make them sound so lovely—you wouldn't *mean* them, my darling!" The first bliss and wonder no longer sustained her. She wept for the frustration she was causing him, and for herself for causing it. She must somehow kill this unlucky love, Hugh must help her kill it, he must stop seeing her, she must simply leave the Cape, run *away*, if he didn't stop. He found himself patiently saying but if he helped her kill it she'd only weep the more, didn't she see that? and she wept in grateful agreement. The sheer confusion of her scruples began to make all her other relationships seem insubstantial to her compared to Hugh, even impossible to feel as once she had felt them. Love in particular was becoming so completely Hugh that it was being Cope's wife she found strange—"I don't really *remember* any more how I felt about him when we were married," she lamented. She lost two pounds more.

Her wretchedness was so endearing that Hugh found himself flattered into being amiably upset too. There were times, in the unconscious campaign of counter-seduction her tears were confronting him with, when he disentangled himself and left her plus étonné de son propre cœur, as Stendhal put it, que de tout ce qui lui arrivait.

Then finally, one lamenting afternoon, he asked her how long did she expect either of them to go on putting up with all this.

". . . I know," she said meekly. "I know we can't."

"And known it for days," he said, getting to his feet. "So come on," as if what they were talking about were something very brisk and kind, and pulled her up too.

She said, ". . . your bed then not mine," in a doleful and docile voice, and let him lead her to his car; and they drove to his cottage without another word.

But, as they drove, he could almost feel her begin to quake. A sort of dread settled over them; the air between them filled with a sense of hovering doom. (He could have shot himself: why in God's name had he ever let this quivering angel of his maneuver him into any such mood-ruining démarche? There were other beds in her damn' cottage; there was a splendid roomy sofa; there was that hearthrug, even! . . .) But sure enough, when they pulled up at his door she put her face in her hands and whispered miserably, "Hugh I can't."

For a moment what came into his head was a grandmother's firm-minded "It isn't what thee wants, it's what's good for thee." But no. Poor angel, he put an arm around her and petted her and said there there, and when it was no, no was what it had to be said it was; and now how about his taking her out to lunch and putting off seducing her till tomorrow.

—But then it was late that same afternoon that he heard

her car drive up again as he was cleaning his brushes in the kitchen, and she walked into his arms without a word.

—First times tend to be too much of an Event. Also, crossing an unknown frontier one proceeds warily, for what are the natives like? This time, too, as a mild nuisance, Hugh found himself thinking critically of Cope's grounding. Still, when late that night she rang him up from her own bed to say good night again, she was murmurous with happiness, all miseries of indecision melted and gone.

—But next morning it was the happiness that was gone. Her voice on the phone was cold with accusation.

"I've betrayed Cope and I've betrayed myself. I can't even understand myself! Or *you,* Hugh! I'm not the *sort* of wife that has affairs! I've never even—"

What'd she mean, "affairs"—he *loved* her!

"Does saying 'I love you' to me make it *not* an affair? Everything I thought about myself's gone! Oh I think it's horrifying to have upset my life so—my darling love how can you treat me like this!" she cried at him, as if making sense.

And when he interrupted this tirade to say he'd be in Wellfleet in ten minutes, she answered drearily, "I don't want to see you. Hugh I can't even look at you, I don't want to see you at *all,* can't you understand?" and hung up.

He of course set out instantly for Wellfleet anyhow.

She met him at the door, barring his way. "Hugh if he finds out I love you, if he even *suspects*, I'll tell him!"

"You out of your head?"

"But *of course* I'd tell him! If he suspects he'll suffer—could I bear to let him do that? It would be letting him down! And with *you*, my darling!"

He thought what did she call going to bed with him? but he managed to say only that he didn't altogether follow the consistencies in all this.

"Are you stupid? If he doesn't suspect that we've—that I love you so, how can he suffer? *I* have to suffer. But I have to.

For being furtive and clandestine and— Can't you understand how *horrified* I am at being an adulteress? I can't even explain myself to myself! You don't even try to understand me!" she cried at him, in a perfect tantrum of woe, and flung into the house.

Sed enim tener ecce Cupido: this is what a love affair with a thoroughly nice girl can be like. So he took a deep breath and followed her in, and, as it turned out, didn't go home again for two days.

—But back, soon enough, came Cope from the edified Balkans; and at the party Caroline gave for his return she was so meek and husbandward that Hugh she seemed barely to look at. This infuriated and alarmed him. ("I wasn't 'jealous' goddammit," he told me, later. "Who's jealous of husbands? What I was, was *outraged*. . . .") He left early, grim. And drove back to Chatham snarling an Ovidian

> "Why should this uninvited swine
> Enjoy you, blast him, now you're mine!"

in no more worthwhile a state of mind than if he'd been sixteen.

But there on his pillow (how under the sun had the angel managed to put it there?) he found a letter:

Please, my darling, don't worry about me, and I will try not to worry about you. We will both have our horrifying and miserable moments—but is that new to us by now. Somehow this time *will* be gotten through. I love you, I am bursting with it, and it is lovely and terrible—you have made me more warm and alive and my human self than any other woman can ever feel. I need you because I love you. And that's what "I love you" means today.

He was stricken. Could any man on earth have foreseen such a tenderness of consolation? He charged out his cottage door and shot away in his car back to the party, almost laughing aloud.

—But now they had the tedium of being circumspect—and sometimes they were not. At one evening party, discussing a next day's picnic with Caroline and their hostess, he suddenly heard his voice *telling* Caroline what to bring, in a tone of proprietorship for anybody to hear; and in an instant saw the woman's eyes widen at him, then glance swiftly at Caroline's face, and then, with a new light in them, back into his. All she said, presently, was a bland, "You know, you two are perfectly beautiful together." But that was merely luck.

It was not until college opened again that they felt free. What Hugh then did with his time, an occasional seminar aside, nobody could verify. Caroline and he could spend long hours together, at this or that rendezvous, without its ever occurring to anybody that they were missing, much less missing at the same time—parting (to his amusement) with the lovers' precautionary phrase she had borrowed for them from *The Golden Bowl*, "What shall you say . . . that you've been doing?"

They could plan. They could meet at parties unfrustrated and hence at ease: life was always an enchanted *soon*. . . . They even managed a night now and then in Boston. Her ordinary daily life was what now seemed to her, she told him, a secondary kind of, reality, like scenery on a darkened stage in a deserted theatre, where she found herself walking through a part she could still just remember she had once played.

And as the college year went on they evolved rituals. She asked him what she should wear to parties. She betrayed her dearest friends' most compromising secrets to him ("I promised her I wouldn't tell anybody ever. Will you *promise* never to tell?"). They discussed money. She refused to make love on the maid's day out. He balanced her cheque-book for her.

But the scheduling of adultery in a college town is not an exercise for laymen. The circumspection itself unnerved her.

"My darling love I'm afraid of all sort of things I'm afraid I haven't even *thought* of! And I have to *act!*—even if we've just been making love and I'm in that haze about you I have to act! When what I want is for everything I do to show I love you. And *you* are so careful and cool when you look at me at parties that my heart *sinks!* You don't even look as if you loved me! And how can I be sure you still do?"

She developed wild superstitions. Their meetings had omens. If a day of planned rendezvous began well, this was the Bona Dea reassuring her; if something happened to prevent a meeting, that too was the Bona Dea, watching over them—the rendezvous (for reasons they of course couldn't know) would have been terribly, even fatally, dangerous. "We're being indulged, whether you think so or not," she would tell him, with a convert's serenity. "For all we know, my darling, we've been saved again and again. . . ."

So at last, perhaps inevitably in the course of things, one night late in the spring she asked Cope for a divorce.

She and Hugh had spent the night before in Boston. She had driven back in dreamy reminiscences of everything they had done and said, her whole body a remembrance; and when, that evening, there was Cope amiably saying come to bed, "suddenly I just couldn't," she told Hugh on the phone.

"I didn't know myself I was going to say it!—divorce I mean. But when he said come to bed, I— How *could* I let him? So I just—I said I hoped he'd forgive me but I didn't love him any more, I knew it was awful but I'd fallen in love and please would he divorce me. So he said *who with?* in a terrible voice, so I said nobody he knew, a man I'd met last summer. So he said in a snarly sort of way then I'd been having an affair, *that* was why I went to Boston? and I said no I *had not!* oh my love what else was there to say? when it was you! So then he—oh Hugh it went on and on and on and finally he said all right *all right* he'd divorce me, by this time he ought to be used to his parade of fluttering capricious love-simple temporary wives! and I went into the guest room and slept there. So I'm still all yours. And I'll stay that way, are you glad?"

He said he'd be with her in five minutes, and took off.

She was picking out her books from Cope's shelves. Three or four stacks already stood on the long library table. She dropped a handful of volumes and ran to him, crying, "I locked my door!" and clung to him.

But when he approvingly kissed her she pulled away. "Oh Hugh we can't, not *now*. I mean now he knows. I feel too odd to, can't you see that anyway? I almost don't know who I am all over again. My darling I woke up so early, it was hardly sunrise even, and I lay there saying to myself, out loud, over and over, I could hardly believe it, 'I'm not Cope's wife any more, I'm not Coplestone Colville's *wife!* I'm Hugh Tatnall's faithful mistress, is who I am!' I felt terribly light and free, I felt like dancing! I got up and dressed and crept out of the house and walked and walked in that cool early-dawn light, just feeling *new*. Then I began to feel shy—my darling love, almost as if I'd just met you! so I came home and made break— No you must not kiss me, please Hugh not in his house, not *now*, I don't care if you do think I'm superstitious, you have to go, don't you see you must? until I'm not *here!*"

She went to a classmate's in Amherst for the night; and next afternoon Cope, with the grim gallantry of experience, drove her to her sister's in Cambridge.

So at last she was Hugh's.

But at a damn' inconvenient distance; and this at once led to nonsensical telephone dialogue.

"What are you doing, are you working? My darling I know I shouldn't interrupt you. But I long for you so! And all evening I've been imagining I'm jealous, do you think that's silly?"

He said even damn' silly.

"Are you stupid? All your students are in love with you,

do you dare deny it? Some slinky little thing could *this next minute* come languishing in with her drawings!"

He said but—

"As if any of you ever say No! Have you ever said it? *Have you?*"

So after a couple of weeks of this sort of thing he said to her dammit look, the term was practically speaking over, why shouldn't he cut his last seminars short and take off with her for Portofino right away, she like to?—next week why not!

She was silent.

Mildly surprised, he said but surely it couldn't take her more than a week to pack, for God's sake, could it? Portofino—

She said, ". . . *live* with you?" in an uncertain voice.

She afraid it might lead to seduction or something?

Silence.

He said, taken aback, but what *was* this?

". . . Everybody would know!"

But good god, he said, nobody did, right out practically in plain view, day after day on the Cape!

"Oh Hugh *of course* they'd know! People drop *in!* And all your Italian friends would— Hugh, Italy's *Italy!* And then it would all get back here!"

Was she making this hair-raising fuss, he demanded, totally baffled, about nothing more than a little *gossip?*

". . . and what would come of it," she said, in a voice of tears.

And go she absolutely would not! Nor did Hugh it seems ever get a lucid reason out of her. Long afterward, once, he told me he'd had to conclude it was probably nothing but a cockeyed sense of decorum. Or of responsibility. "Or some idiotic other kind of behavior about her damn' husband's feelings—people saying 'What, his still undivorced wife living openly with a *colleague?*' and the like. Who ever knows anyhow?"

—Enchantment will for a time go on. But suppose one has happened to ask oneself toward what? . . . Often in the dusk of that summer's evenings, perhaps, Caroline would lean on the balustrade of her sister's balcony and watch the last gulls winging dully seaward down the Charles as night came on, and all her life would seem to her planless and bereft. And Hugh, like Cope, was a quarter-century older than she was.

So who can suppose he was surprised, home that winter from a leisurely visit to his London and Paris agents, at her telling him that she was, well, she was thinking of— Oh how could she make him see that really it was the best thing for them both!—she was thinking of marrying a very nice, a very *kind* Harvard ecologist, and would he perhaps, oh please, still love her enough to understand? . . .

"And by god Simon d'you know she wouldn't even spend one last consoling night of adieu with me?—*wept* when I reasoned with her!" Hugh was still complaining, months later. "Can you account for such peremptory heartlessness? As if I'd been just any goddam passing affair!"

God help us, I thought, has it never been borne in on him, with some girl or other, that these taperings-off are just a masculine ("but oh sweet not really a *sensible* . . .") romanticism. But all I said was, ah well, he'd gone to the wedding like a gent.

"What's a wedding? Tribal ceremony like any other—you drink what looks like champagne, and in decent families tastes like it too, but you're just drinking potlatch. *Yes* I went! Even behaved well, dammit—even when I kissed *my* angel in the receiving line, and found all I was given to kiss was a cheek!"

V I I

A resonance as of peroration in Taige's voice brought my mind back to the meetinghouse.

. And sure enough, at long oratorical last he had generalized himself to an eloquent final throwaway:

> "... For a little our deathbound
> delight grows high, in a little falls to the dust,
> toppled by a Heed I quail at.
>   What are we, or are not?—a shadow's phasm
> is Man,"

he intoned nobly, turned, stepped gravely back to his place on the facing benches, and sat down.

—Pindar. That Homer of the ho-hum. I glanced at Camilla: been dozing. Very practical. And at Persis—and was gratified to see she'd responded to Taige's sonorities with tears. Like a good girl: that was what I'd fetched her for, high Pindaric nonsense or not.

—Except, finally, what *is* one to say of the dead? Listing a man's qualities reduces the throbbing human animal, the everyday sociable sardonic friend, to anonymity: *tolerant generous loyal* are not the predicates of a unique being but of that universal bore Everyman. And *wise* is no better: all it signifies is having sat and amiably listened while assorted fools made up their minds aloud at you in detail.

Why defame a dead friend with the truth about him in any case! What business of Hugh's gossiping mourners, for instance, were things like that cache of libertine mementos I had come across in the palazzo in Florence?—in a locked drawer of his uncle's red-and-gold Venetian Baroque secretary, a great wadded-in mass of old letters, photographs, bloc-notes, journals, a sketch or two—a midden of nameless litter that bulged up out of the drawer the moment I pulled it open, and sent the top sheets of it sailing and slithering in handfuls across the waxed red tiles of the salotto floor. In what innocence I picked the first sheaf up!

And was stunned. Could the entire drawer be this giggling

record of a quarter-century of campus assignations? Amorous little notes that had been sneaked, breathless, under doors; slipped tenderly under pillows; stuffed wildly down the fronts of pajama trousers, shrieking and giddy with laughter; tucked into pockets of lovingly laundered shirts in chests of drawers. Notes signed ("à *Toi*") with what flattering sighs, with what submissive redesignings of a persona ("Schmutzling—and I found out what it means, so there!"). Signatures too of total unmaidenliness—a Pill scotch-taped on, a chastely beribboned little lock of unambiguous curls, a magenta-lipsticked *Scroomie?* squirming with archness. I love you I loff you I loave you I louve you I L*o*v*e you.

Or, for a plus-ça-change, that sentence on the letterhead of Northampton's extremely stern-minded young lady psychiatrist: "Don't be beastly to Blossom—Blossom doesn't like it beastly."

Why under heaven had of all people *Hugh* stored this hilarious gabble away? Against what conceivable ruins? What had it even to do with the fact of Hugh, as in the unmasked and lawless privacy of his mind he himself must have known himself? ...

The drawer did, here and there, I found, hold random bits of respectable sanity. There was for example, near the top, a lighthearted postcard of Restoration adieu:

> Once on a time a nightingale
>   To changes prone,
> Unconstant, fickle, whimsicall,
>   (A female one) ...
>   Addio, amoreggiato!

Or again, such touches of civilized tradition as a colorphoto of a sweetly laughing Nadezhda in a sun-flooded noonday angle of the torricella terrace at Portofino, mixing a glittering salad in a blue faenze bowl, at the long table down whose top twin black-and-gold scagliola dragons coiled languidly toward the far end laid for lunch for two, the turquoise sea foaming and adazzle behind her far below, through the dark thickets of cypress and olive—che bella che indimenticabile ragazza! black hair piled high on her stylish head gleaming and glossy in the sun, cameo profile turned half toward him; sweetly laughing; sweetly indulging him with her beauty.

As Taige had said: all what long years now past and gone. . . .

—Yes; but what note of elegy could one hear in the choral echoes of that drawer as a whole? Hardly half an inch down, for instance, I came on Hugh's wriggling affectionate Rachel.

Whom I remembered with unusual disapprobation. She had a long swishing mane of blue-black hair and wore a different set of bangles each time one saw her. The moment she'd spotted Hugh she'd loved him. She had, it's true, just got herself engaged to some helpless instructor at Yale. But she loved him *too*, she explained to Hugh: he was her betrothed *husband* —would Hugh have her marry without love? She spent so much of that term in Hugh's bed that she nearly lost her place on the Dean's List. But she didn't *actually* lose it, did she? *Well* then!

I concede that many a Smith girl might have thought this conduct on the exotic side. Or, depending on temperament, on the idealistic. But would any of them have indulged their daydreams with the sequel?—for what did Rachel do but come dancing back from her honeymoon to spend the second term as lovingly in Hugh's bed, and as assiduously, as she had spent the first.

Even Hugh was staggered. He did, for a time, try like a gent to rally his good manners and explain to her (her naked young arms round his neck) that after all one can't just— One doesn't perhaps quite so *soon* simply— He was never allowed to finish. Tears. Great mournful eyes. Heartbreak.

What in God's thundering name, Hugh bayed at me, was a lifetime's devoted attention to womanly démarches, if he now found them baffling his declining years like *this!*

(I must have laughed at him for a month. *Poor* old bastard, what a shock! Why, nobody who hadn't taught at the best women's colleges would ever have *conceived* such things could happen!)

—Yet I must often myself have known some of this drawer's seraphic little simpletons and never once dreamed what visions of the burgeoning feminine soul were being denied me! My simple doting faith in women as women, I supposed, their hair-raising mélange of sense and sensibility— how my simplemindedness had sheltered me! I gave the drawer up, daunted. The angelic babble was unreadable.

The journals too I soon gave up—stupri vetus consuetudo, Sallust would have said, a resounding phrase meaning "a long practice of seduction" or "many years' habituation to delinquency," depending on your frame of mind when you translate it. There were, of course, here too, amusing exceptions. I particularly remember a note on Persis, apparently the first time she'd come to see him, about admission to his seminar:

> Great wide innocent green eyes (gold & virid?) as full of wonder as if she'd just been making love while having what she was doing gently explained to her as she did it. Winterhalter's young *Princesse de Morny* at Compiègne! I see Winterhalter's point! Said to me, "Oh people are such mysteries, Mr. Tatnall, why a girl can look at the boy she's been seeing [Christ what a verb!] and just turn *cold* with not knowing what he's really like, oh how lonely and despairing it can be!"

What business had biography with any of this? For think what variations of unreality this preposterous drawer showed even me, a lifelong friend, I had mistaken for familiar fact. What scholarly nonsense, accordingly, art historians of the future could be expected to make of the contents. For aren't data data? Isn't Hugh Tatnall himself the unimpeachable final factual word on Hugh Tatnall? *Poor* Hugh!—guggenheim'd and transmuted, the minutiae of his misconduct sorted and reassembled to make sense, the whole random picaresco of his loves scrupulously fitted into whatever the psychaesthetics in fashion held his canvases to mean, Hugh would rise from the dead a learned Project, rational, exhaustive, fact-packed, and unrecognizable. And undefended.

I burned the lot, except for the picture of Nadezhda.

—But if my bonfire had saved Hugh from the indignities of future speculation, still how account for his keeping such stuff in the first place? Notes and reminders for Casanovan memoirs struck me as out of character. Incidental detail for a formal autobiography was likelier, to be worked up perhaps as ironic running commentary on the follies he had seen and lived through and put up with: a kind of memento sapere. Or was it nothing but his casualness?—and the stuff had simply so little importance for him that he'd never so much as got around to deciding what to do with it. That was in character, certainly. But then also in character, it occurred to me, would have been a memento sapere sardonically addressed to himself ("a little common *sense* next time for once goddammit! . . .") —for the offhand follies he let himself in for were sometimes as plain to him as they were to me.

His affair, for example, with that mocking young daimon Maura Mac a'Bhoghainn: almost anybody would have known better on sight. Young women writers can be pure hazard; and to make it worse, this one was as talented as she was dangerous. The college thought her perhaps an even more gifted undergraduate poet than Plath had been. And she was more precocious: not only had her first volume of poems come out when she was still a sophomore, but the Eastern literary establishment had reviewed it with respectful discursiveness. It was a collection of some forty flaunting and tumescent lyrics entitled *Triskelion*, a Celtic symbol with a Greek name but no language needed to make the point, the three legs being self-translating. Several individual poems had titles on the same principle, and if "Trismyriakis" isn't in *Liddell and Scott* its meaning '30,000 times' is clear enough, times what not having to be stated. I doubt if Hugh ever read any of them.

Yet what could he have been in ignorance of?—the book had been a newspaper scandal as well. A Boston reviewer had been so outraged by a short set of lyrics with the wicked title "Noctuary for an Impotent Lover" that she denounced not only them and their title, but the volume, its concept, its message, and (gifted or not) its shameless author as well; and when the academic community weighed in with intellectual defense, even the explications de texte turned into publicity. Was this young woman to be seen as Lib, anti-Lib, or just a merciless young free-lance sexist deriding our national calamity? Further, which of the six contemporary sexes was this text addressed to? (Or, perhaps, aimed at? . . .) And how should we assess the style: was it high anti-mandarin, or just vulgar?

Not Hugh's type.

Also, unluckily, he happened on her at a dangerous moment. One spring night he had gone into a late-open snack bar for a bite. It was toward midnight; the place was empty except for a fry-cook behind the counter and, at a table, the girl, a suitcase on the floor beside her. Hugh sat down and made campus conversation: what was she doing with that bag?—off weekending in the middle of the week?

Oh, weekends (she'd said, in a soft Irish-sounding drawl), who bothered about weekends, did he? Nah, she was leaving. Leaving college. Till she felt like coming back. If she did.

Classes boring her that much?

She'd answered, letting her tawny eyes rest on him as if his civilities amused her, oh, it wasn't classes, what were classes. She was just running off, was all. Did he mind?

So he'd asked what from?

Had it got to be "from" something? she said, as if contemptuously; and then, in a voice so indolently erotic it startled him, "I'm going adrift," she said, eyes in his. "Anywhere I please, Mr. Traditional Tatnall. And any *how* ..."

The derisiveness, not to say the easy arrogance, of any such provocation as that should have turned any man wary. The best one can say for Hugh, probably, is that he was so used to invitation that he could no longer tell when it was challenge. So in his folly he said well then if she was off come have one for the road with him, wouldn't she?—"and by god Simon the coldhearted young trollop was in my bed before her glass was more than sipped from!"

She wasn't beautiful: her face he said was "like a sleepy cat's." But never *never* had he had such a— Well, in two days he was *hooked*, and she'd stayed with him four. . . .

Then he had woken, in the first early paleness of dawn, alone.

In an instant he knew the status, the depths, of his outrage. He leaped from his forsworn bed and ran through his rooms half-deranged. She was not there; she was gone; her suitcase was gone; she was *gone*. He threw on his clothes and charged savagely out into the dawn silence of the streets groaning aloud with the affront of it. It was still barely light; as he raced in rage toward the bus station the first cool streaks of sunrise were no more than a chiaroscuro in the sky.

He was in time. The early bus had not even rolled in: the dusky slab of the loading-lot stretched out blank and deserted in the graying light, and he made out her solitary figure at the shadowy end of the ticket shed.

She was sitting on her suitcase, head leaned indolently back against the shed wall, the smoke of her cigarette curling slowly up into the still dawn air—watching him come, her long gaze coolly expecting him. He jolted to a halt before her, shaken and panting, too winded to speak; and there she sat, looking up into his face with a kind of indulgent mockery, waiting—

unconcernedly waiting—for whatever his fury or his anguish would decide to say.

But at last, "Why, look at you," she drawled, in amusement, "up and all sexy so bright and early . . . ," and with an easy sweep of her body she was up and smoothly against him, palm stroking his cheek, voice of honey murmuring, "And you *missed* me? . . ." softly laughing into his distorted face. "Did he wake up alone by his great self and miss me then? oh but what a pet he was to miss her!" she crooned, all teasing caress. "And when all he wanted was so easy, so *easy*. . . ."

But stay she would not.

"I like you, *pet* pet," she murmured that night, very late, sprawled on him all anyhow in the tumbled bed, rosy tongue delicately tasting him, lips grazing and smoothing, "I like you I like you, all so yummy and pretty. And ooooooh how I love screwing. But I told you. I am *Me*. And I'm going adrift. Because *I* want to, see? Don't you listen? And I am not to be chased after! What d'you expect me to do, pet—*love* you or something?"

But, shortly, he had talked her into going abroad with him. He had shown her Italy. She wanted to see Tangiers. He got her an abortion in Denmark. She recuperated in Ireland. He did no painting at all.

I was appalled at him. "Didn't even paint her?" I said.

"Refused to sit."

" '*Refused*'!"

"Said she was an artist herself, not a damn' model! Wrote me a nasty poem called 'Lay-Figure' to prove it."

"But holy god," I said, "how long did this preposterous— Her family think she was here still?"

How'd *he* know what story the unfeeling young slut had told them? Father was some grim Gogmagog of a Catholic-ward police captain in Boston. Used to beat her with a strap, she said. Maybe the black-avised old aurochs had a point!

I said ah well we can't all expect to limit our Boston infatuations to Brahmins. Not that tampering with the iron chastity of Celtic womanhood was an alternative I'd have thought *he*'d have hit on. But then what, after Europe? Back to Boston?

What else? He'd got her an apartment.

He'd *set up* a poetess?!—like a show-girl for God's sake?

Did *I* classify what I took to bed sociologically? And anyhow, he'd snarled, trollop or not, for months she's certainly been *his* kind of bedfellow, and he hers. Even when, presently, she'd now and then put a visit off, weekends, her excuses had been reasonable enough: even at a last minute, reasonable. That soft voice over the phone was an illusion of reality. And if he didn't paint her, what of it?

All this I'd known about, and thought pretty poorly of, for half the semester. But curae est sua cuique voluptas—you *see* to what you fancy, and what did I know about poetesses anyway. Maybe in bed they're not so scary. Possibly he even knew what he was doing. Or, with this one, was in luck. God behaving as He sees fit to, anything is possible.

But unluckily luck runs out. It happened an autumn evening a cool young houri of a sophomore in my Ancient Greek Religions course had asked to come consult me about her term paper. But she had been drooping her unmaidenly eyelids at me for a month, so I concluded that her demure "Would it be all right if I came round *after* dinner, Professor Shipley?" was a ladylike fair warning, and I was to make up my mind. But we had no more than finished the ritual discussion of her paper ("Orphism at Eion-on-Strymon"—not that anyone knows anything much about Orphism anywhere else either), and I was admiringly watching her work her way along the transitional sequences, when there came a buffet of a knock on my door and in stomped Hugh, almost before my young huntress could stifle a shriek and spring away.

Hugh lifted his eyebrows at us, murmured something about consultations at *this* hour, what next what next, was my brandy still in the kitchen? and stalked pointedly past.

So the girl had to go. Though at the door she turned for a sultry moment, poised hand on knob, eyes saying what she thought of my incompetent hospitality, then with a deadly flash toward the kitchen and an "It's-been-awfully-helpful-Professor-Shipley-you-were-terribly-kind!" she was gone.

Hugh came strolling back in, asking where in fact *was* my good brandy kept goddammit anyway!

I said it had never been in the kitchen in the first place; was in the tantalus; always was always had been; and whose tottering virtue had he thought he was preserving, hers or mine?

Then I saw he was seething.

And what a story: He and his Mac a'Bhoghainn had had a weekend feast planned. He'd got a couple of twenty-ounce Maine lobsters, for an homard Delmonico. She was to have port and cream in, and a Meursault. All arranged. As often before. Except that, this time, she and her flouting subconscious had miscalculated the day.

His key therefore had opened her door onto a disarray, a locker-room squalor, beyond civilized sanity. The apartment looked west, and now, through the living-room windows he faced, the last sunset light fell in great fading bars of ocher and cadmium red across a coffee table slopped with the leavings of a lovers' breakfast. Detail by detail his eye took the sleazy still life in, his minutely concentrated painter's eye—the smeared gray-whites of the plates, the highlights in the dull-umber dregs of a coffee cup, the glint of a gutted sardine tin, a yellow sludge of lipsticked butter on a gob of toast. A bath towel, still damp, hung limp down the back of a chair; another lay in a wad on the floor by the sofa.

The slattern anarchy of the kitchen was worse: what looked like half a week's unwashed dishes stood in the motionless scum of the sink. He was stupefied.

Sack of lobsters dangling from his fingers, he went into the bedroom. "And *there* by god," he burst out at me, "I saw the psychopathic disorder of her for what it is!"—the disheveled bed, stained pillows all anyhow, a torn slip in a silky heap at the bed's foot with a pair of dirty socks, half a dozen empty beer cans and a rosary under the table de chevet—"Simon goddammit I was looking into cold chaos on every side, a total attestation to *what* all these months I'd thought I was living on...." He was paralyzed with apperception.

Then he gave a great laugh of rage, hurled the lobsters headlong onto that wallowed-in and unspeakable bed, and came savagely away.

—I can still hardly believe I heard such stuff. Or that it was Hugh Tatnall I was listening to, whose charged and luminous canvases of girls (he'd once blandly said) made Matisse's odalisques look as if they were "right out of a plush maison de passe in the Bourse quarter." And the problem not even a problem!—simply that a libertine had come up against a female libertine and, naturally, she'd out-libertined him. And why leave her two perfectly good lobsters?

But one cannot confront a lifelong friend with the unkindness of the self-evident. Humane diversion was what was called for, not the horrors of common sense.

Still, I thought, whether he had come to me for disabused advice or just as a handy audience for the rhetoric of moral resentment, he was in fact suffering from what Ovid once urbanely called indignae regna puellae, "the reign of an unworthy girl," and among Ovid's detailed recipes for getting oneself out of subjection I remembered one that was as good as written for Hugh's case. "Have two girls," says Ovid. With two infatuations you're unlikely to be more than half-infatuated with either, et voilà.

So I said to Hugh (in sympathy) outrage by god I agreed it was. And unprecedented. They go sweetly to bed with us or they don't; we call the gods down to witness their perfidies or we don't have to; but *this* one he'd got hold of was both kinds at once—what was the world coming to!

All the same, what had got into *him*? Did he expect the

complaisancies of an offhand carnality to last longer in a young poetess than in one of those fifty-five kilos of young finishing-school experimenters his seminar was usually full of? And, this term, was as full of as ever? Was I to believe he hadn't even looked at them? Had he gone lazy on us? What were seminars *for?* ...

He snorted at me. I meant another girl for God's sake, and as *therapy?* What sort of heartless inattention to a girl's feelings would *that* be?—what kind of insensibility was I crediting him with? And he didn't want another girl anyhow, blast it— he wanted *this* one!

I said he dejected me. Had he got so used to just taking what was handy that he'd got so he couldn't deal with what wasn't? And the plain fact was, he wasn't going to be able to stand this coolheaded young tramp of his much longer in any case:

Entre de si beaux bras de *tels* emmerdements?

—I said he was too damn' spoiled to! Women had been enchantedly building up his amour propre for him from his uncle's pets on, and it wasn't going to put up now with anything else. *Or* stick around.

So would he give over? And run over his seminar class list with—if not therapy—at least agréments in mind?

—It took less time than I expected; quite soon in fact I got him off into the night, if not convinced about the seminar, at least committed to a campus survey. From the door I called encouragingly after him not to forget Ovid's advice on lovers' diets too ("Don't eat onions or cabbage. Nibble at a bunch of rue now and then."). I went back into my rooms laughing, much pleased with myself. And with Ovid.

Well, yes. But just at that self-satisfied moment there came a light tap at my door; and never mind Ovid on the subject, there was my term-paper angel again.

Who smiled blandly into my eyes, murmuring, "I don't *like* people to interrupt me, do you either?" and stepped sweetly in.

"And anyhow I made up a French alexandrine about you while I was waiting," she went on, as if conversationally, pulling off her mittens and unbuttoning her coat. "It's sort of cute and surrealist. Do you understand French, Professor Shipley? I mean, spoken French? Anyhow, it goes

Que j'ajoute a ton Un les zéros de mon cœur—

d'you like it? I thought I could have it say toi to you in poetry, they all do," she explained smoothly, dropping her coat in sheerest ballet onto a chair. "Except oh, though, do you really mind?" she asked, suddenly all eyes at me. "Because I hope really you don't—don't maybe *you*? . . . ," and came serenely across the room toward whatever I was going to do about it.

So naturally I said, "I even understand unspoken English," and that was how, on a night of damage to a friend's enchantment, I acquired Hildegarde.

Or Hildegarde me, depending on one's Darwinian assumptions. Though, either way, I hardly know whether to call it a blessing or a luxury—a light-headed and airily self-willed young luxury, I admit, but what an impiety toward the Bona Dea or Whoever to find fault, the coquetting body poised on its slender elbows over me, the voice delightedly teasing, "Do you love me? But do you *love* me? . . ." eyes alight with amusement at the sheer wanton inconsequence of the parody.

Though why she fancied me? Discussion was not for Hildegarde. Her eyes would turn mocking and demure, her body wriggle and flounce: no answers. Or in pure frivolous ambiguity, "Oh but think if I *loved* you!"—and that was that.

"And anyway oh ptah," she would say patronizingly. "Most of the girls don't even *start* deciding to seduce a professor till they're juniors or seniors—*so silly!* And time-wasting! You aren't pleased *I'm* practical?"

Among her amenities, she kept me documented in campus scandal, in particular the fatuities she amused herself by tantalizing this or that gulping colleague of mine into. Her favorite at one time was our yearning Sociology chairman. She would report, sweetly smirking, "Harry the Pad discussed frigidity this morning in lecture. Looking right *at* me. Oh how sad!"

Harry was known as "The Pad" to distinguish the area of his quantified concerns from that of a departmental colleague called Harry "d'Urgence." Not that d'Urgence was around the campus often enough to make a distinction essential: he spent much of his time rushing up and down the Eastern seaboard testifying fervently before legislative committees, or vaticinating on learned panels, in anguished support of downtrodden causes. The Pad was our *relaxed* sociologist. Or had been, until his besotment with Hildegarde.

Who would mockingly report to me, trailing light fingertips along my spine, "I'm a college-girl love-object, did you know that? Harry the Pad said so. See why you adore me?"

I said 'said so'?

"Well, he did! After class. And patted my bottom."

"Nonsense."

"Well, he wanted to!"

"Interpersonally, this was?"

"Oh you're always so old-sneery about sociology!"

"You have to be told why?—in bed with a humanist?"

"You're just kind of old-fashioned, I guess, aren't you," she said, sliding a flowerlike hand under my belly. "*Sunch a pinny!* How am I to explain you to my roommate?"

"No cachet?"

But "Why won't you turn *over?*" she complained, collapsing tenderly onto me, tongue-tip in my ear. "Because why not explicitize some parameters of interpersonal *humanist* struc-

turing, then—don't you *want* to? Aren't you ever going to Be
Lovely again?"

Hugh had once caught her eye at a faculty-student tea.
"Ooooh how beautiful! And I had him talking to me a *long*
time. He wanted me to model for him!" Should she add him to
her Circe's stable? Maybe she ought to explore him, she said in
her love-making voice, what did I think?

"Let him sink his great yellowing dentures in you?"

"Well, you're all of you always telling us we should broaden
our horizons, aren't you?"

"So you're going to cuckold me with a damn' painter!"

"Going to *what*?"

"Cuckold."

"What's that?"

I said, "God help me, Hildegarde, have you survived the
batterings of reality all the way into sophomore year at Smith
without acquiring the basic vocabulary of your lifework? Go
look it up in the Concise Oxford!"

"Way off in the study? Why should I!"

"You're at Smith College to learn!"

"What *you*'ve been teaching me? Hoh!"

"Get going, you illiterate siren."

"I don't know how you spell your stupid word anyway!"

"Get out of my bed, dammit, and look it up!"

"You're so *spoiled*," she grumbled.

She came back saying, "... oh," slanting her eyes at me.

"Horizon broadened?"

"Well, I knew it in French, or practically, so there!"

"Spoken French?"

She pounced down on me, spluttering laughter. And romped.

—With what cool efficiency, too, she moved in on me. I
hadn't *really* decided, had I, on my summer plans? Because
she herself (she explained, fingers delicately rearranging my
hair—"All this graying charm: so *sexy!*") she herself was
going to be on the Normandy coast. Because Mummy was

renting this manoir of a cousin of hers's. Not actually *on* the coast, sort of back in the country a few kilometers: *undisturbed*. Deauville was nearish, but nobody had to socialize. Mummy said the place wasn't what it was anyway.

"And you've thought of some villa near by for me."

"Mm."

"Where you can keep a ladylike eye on me."

"Mm."

"Some jeune fille à tout faire go with this place?"

"Well naturally I told Mummy one of my most presentable professors was looking for a summer research assistant."

"Who wouldn't mind working late?"

"But silly, a *live-in* one!"

I was brought up to be taken aback by this sort of thing. I found myself saying but had her mother—

"Well *naturally* I told her how sort of terribly stuffy and correct you were, she could have you to lunch and see for herself. Why, you were just *traditional*, I said."

One is reduced to the clichés of parental guidance.

"But what do you want me to do all summer then, Simon darling?" she asked, all innocence. "Sleep with some *boy*?"

—Years, since then. Other entrancements too; other échanges de deux fantaisies. Other illusions. Yet Hildegarde still seems to me, the distortions of time and tenderness aside, an irreproachable demonstration of what the Bona Dea presumably has in view; and if there is always folly to offset, I should argue we offset it with attachment. Nor do the pruderies of Freudian explanation explain. Freud has his theological uses; but the straightforwardnesses of love were not his specialty, and his experience was with those who had not found love humane.

By Hildegarde's senior year, at any rate, that lighthearted Norman summer had little by little become a ménage, and on the glowing final June morning of her graduation our eyes silently said so to each other across the formal distance that

lay between us, I in the robed and solemn ranks of the faculty
on the rostrum, she in her alphabetical place among her class-
mates out below. Afterwards, too, I walked back to my rooms
thinking how empty now, how silent, I might for a good time
feel they had become. I even found myself remembering a
mulatto lament that Malraux had been moved by in the
Caribbean—

> Doudou à moi elle est partie
> Hélas hélas c'est pour toujours.

For how primitive my desolation!—and for how many hundreds of irrecoverable dawns by then! the last sleepy love-
making before she'd leave so long-familiar, so wedded, a ritual
by now that even on this final morning we had hardly behaved
as if, this time, it was farewell.

Nor was it quite. I heard a car roll up to my curb, and she
sprang out and was up my walk and in, cool and elegant in a
summer-linen suit I'd never seen, lightly announcing, "Well I
have to just *race*, Daddy's out there fuming as it is!"

I managed to say but I thought we'd decided—

"*Yes I know*—only is that any reason I can't come say
goodbye to you with clothes on for once?"

But at that flippant pretext, her gaze—helplessly—flickered
for an instant past me to the open bedroom door, and through
it to the bed, a pillow still dented where she'd left it in the cool
quiet of dawn so few hours before, and when her eyes came
back to mine they were stricken.

I could think of nothing to say. What was there to meet that
look of wordless woe that wouldn't sound like the valediction
it had to be? I started an assuaging—

"I *know!*" she said fiercely. "I saw you looking at me. At
Commencement. I looked at you too, oh I never took my eyes
off you. Oh Simon suppose there isn't ever going to be anybody, in all my life ever again, like you. . . ."

Too much to hope for perhaps I should have answered; something light and false like that; something faithless-hearted for us both. Something practical, even—simple et sensé comme au grand jour. But after three years like those we had lived, how?

She said shakily, "Are you going to be sad?"

"Both of us are."

"You're not helping."

"Helping doesn't help."

In a soft wail she said, "I never thought it was going to feel like this. My darling I'm *in mourning* for you! And oh Simon I don't even dare kiss you, I'll have to make conversation with Daddy all the way home, and if I—if you—"

She choked. But then she lifted her hand, kissed the tips of her fingers, and touched them miserably to my lips. "So there, anyhow!" she whispered. Then one last blinding, endless look, and she'd whirled on her heels, gasping, and was gone.

—It was not till the end of summer that I found, in the drawer of the table de chevet, a ring I had given her three years before. It lay on a scribbled note:

Ne peints pas sur ton cœur nos images d'adieu.

Very stylized: ended with an alexandrine, as begun.

V I I I

A stir at my side. Camilla was looking at her watch.

She was right: the hour must be nearly up. The sober overseers on the facing benches would soberly rise, shake hands with each other and with Taige, and soberly end it; and what were any of us likely to say the solemn ritual of our forgathering had done to lift the heaviness of mortality from any heart? Whose heart could I assume was heavy anyhow, except my

own? The rhetoric of Taige's euphemisms had its splendors
and its uses, but, here, every canting colleague had known
what was not being said about what was being said.

Memories I suppose there were. I had had one or two letters
about Hugh's death that seemed to be trying to say so. But
only a note from Nadezhda, sent from Paris the week he died,
had said it as I'd have thought it might decently have been said
by many more:

> I went to St. Sulpice and lit a candle for him. Not to pull him
> out of Hell or indulge him into another life, but to smell the
> burning wick, and see the flicker in the cup.

And to think it had been Nadezhda, of all his girls (he'd told
me, months afterward), who had first made him feel *old*.

—I remember I was biking across campus one June morning, the first time I saw her. I had been away, on a sabbatical.
I heard myself hailed, and there was Hugh with this marvel of
a girl—where on God's bagnio of an earth, I thought as I
wheeled across to them, does the undeserving bastard *find* this
young-goddess loveliness, these marvels? Her black hair shone
in the sun, twirled up into a lustrous topknot à l'italienne, the
lacy patterns of sun and leaf-shadow came and went across
her face like veils of summer light as we stood there, her bare
arm through his, her shoulder lightly against him, her dark
eyes indulgently on his face as he talked, or on mine, with all
the young wariness of beauty, as I answered. She let Hugh and
me talk, learning I suppose how we were with each other, the
climate and the shared landscapes of our friendship: she had
heard from Hugh what I was like, but what was I *like?* . . . I
remember saying to them finally come along have some coffee,
thinking tolerantly enough-of-this-love-making-let's-get-to-the-
table, for in fact they looked as if they hadn't been out of bed
a decent quarter-hour.

I can't say I ever really worked out the aesthetics of their affair entirely. Nadezhda was cool, elegant, exotic, and per-fectly serene. Her serenity had moreover a kind of foreign poise, her family having been some sort of White Russian exiles. The contrast with Hugh's customary operations was an anomaly I couldn't let pass.

"There been some mutation in your charm while I was away?" I asked him. "Grown-*up* girls go for you now?"

A grunt.

"I mean what are you doing with a girl like this one!"

"This an incivility, or felicitation? Kept her from the usual follies, haven't I?"

"You're not a folly?"

He said sarcastically, "Compared to what?"—though for that matter I hardly thought, then, that she knew why she'd acquired him either. I remember saying to her, "What on earth got into as cool an exotic head as yours anyhow!"

"... Exotic thoughts, perhaps?"

"You mean a whim?"

"What a word, Shipley dear!"

"Want me to call it just a ladylike horsing-around?"

"Oh *poor* man," she mocked, patting my cheek, "haven't you ever had anything but Anglo-Saxon girls?"

Though the explanation, I concluded as I came to know her better, was her sense of her own mise en scène. "Does one have to be 'in love'?" she said to me. "Why not just charmed, or enchanted? Parts of me do behave as if they ought to feel frightened, and I think 'Where am I going, and why?' But then—someone's impossibly sweet, and I can't resist. It was a summer romance, and I just stepped into the story."

(And gently expunged a brief earlier enchantedness as she did so. This was a visiting poet, the spring before, who had given three lectures on *Paradise Lost*, and charmed her; she had spent the Easter weekend with him at an old farm the college used as a guest house. That autumn, to lay the ghost, she had taken Hugh there, picnicking. No one was there; the place lay deserted in the sun of early afternoon. They walked ritually around the house, peering in at the blank windows; she described the layout, the kitchen, the fireplaces in the bedrooms upstairs. They poked about in the barn; she indulged him and made love with him in the haymow. It was an exorcism: when, later, they walked in the woods behind, she wept a little, standing in his arms. "Once or twice I glimpsed my other self, the one who'd been there at Easter," she wrote to him later. "But she and I had nothing to exchange. I cried, there in the autumn beauty of the woods, because I didn't feel what I thought perhaps I should. But how easy to share the beauty with you!—and return to a room with *you*, not to Milton's prosody and him. . . .")

—That it should have been *this* girl who caused Hugh's first grim disquiet at the prospect of age could be thought a piece of Bona Dea pleasantry.

It had happened one morning early in their affair. She was in his dressing room, in bra and bikini, doing her hair up into its gleaming topknot in the gilded baroque scrolling of his glass. He was still lounging lazily in their bed, in simple pleasure watching the ballet of her through the open door; and suddenly, in the glass, she caught him gazing.

For an inscrutable moment her eyes held his. Then she made a mouth at him, as if in sweet derision at anything so wanting in savoir-vivre as that kind of stare. ("I suppose I did look, dammit, like some yokel gawking from a hedgerow," he admitted, "though by god what was I doing but gaze in pure aesthetic delight—a sort of awe, Simon!—at the whole sleek flaunting beauty of her!") She finished doing her hair; then, with another moue at him, did her mouth; then her eyelids, and put in her earrings; and finally she slipped into her dressing gown and came in by the bed. She stood there for a moment, looking down at him with indulgence. Then, "How nice to be new," she said gently, and twirled off to make their breakfast.

"And I went in to shave," he told me. "And in the glass—Are you going to understand what I mean, Simon?—in that damn' glass I *saw* my old face!"

He was thunderstruck. One's face does not change: one sees it as a continuum. But not *that* morning—that morning he had seen the young face of beauty in a glass where now the face he saw was his own, and the face it mirrored he saw had aged by more than thirty years.

"—the thirty years there were between us, d'you understand what it is I'm trying to express?" he cried at me. "I'd never seen her face in *my* glass—never seen her face *like that*—and then, a moment or so after, this withering one of my own!..."

—I felt badly for him over this outburst. No doubt man's private pastime is feeling sorry for himself; but hadn't Hugh been through this sort of experience without a pang often before? He had even been so touched by one girl's mournful "Oh if only you were just *ten* years younger . . ." that its solemn absurdity never struck him. But this time, with Nadezhda—and in bafflement perhaps more than in dismay—he had somehow seen the ghost intervene. This may be what ghosts are for: mortal instruction is traditionally their métier. But here, the looming briefness of mortality, its unfactorable elements compounding the predicament of man, had risen up as if before his eyes, deadly and undeniable, and the consolations of philosophy were wanting.

He of course recovered. But it was not long afterward that he painted the oddly inscrutable self-portrait now in the library collection at Princeton, and on the back of it lettered, with a fine brush, a sardonic epigram:

Gristle and bone, too leathery now to please,
Here th' aging painter Tatnall takes his ease—
While the three Graces, with a teen-age blush,
Sneak out behind him tiptoe, tittering *Hush*. . . .

—And now I thought too of what only that morning, from Persis, I had learned about his last months, in Italy.

I had fetched her to the funeral from her departmental supervisor's, a languid blue-eyed Norwegian sculptress who had a studio in the country beyond Middlefield, an ancient farm now long abandoned and overgrown, where she worked on weekends. She had taken Persis with her, possibly for a report on her research in Italy, possibly (with Hugh in mind) from curiosity.

No one was in sight when I drove in. A woods road, ruts already deep in the soft dust of summer, led in from the highway past a decaying barn to a Bauhaus-rustic pavilion squatting dogmatically in the sun beyond. I went up and banged at the knocker. There was a scuttering of feet inside, the door leaped open, and there, a solemn little golden dream in studious horn-rims and tousled pajamas, and instantly aghast at me, stood Persis.

She uttered a squeak of stricken decorum, whipping off her glasses and desperately smoothing her hair.

"Oh Professor Shipley oh how *awful*, is it already—oh *dear!*" she quavered, in loveliest dismay. "I didn't somehow expect you'd be so—I didn't realize the *time!* and to find me— OH DEAR!" she wailed, scuttling off ahead of me into a wide functionally bleak living room. "I'll be ready in five *minutes*, Professor Shipley, if you'll just— My adviser's not— She went to— *Honestly* only five minutes, Professor!" and fled off into some farther depths of the house.

She then immediately came darting back in.

"Oh while you're waiting would you perhaps like—I mean maybe you knew there was this scholarly article on those sketches Hugh did of all those Roman ruins in Asia Minor, it tried to prove he was parodying Piranesi stylistically?—so I mean while I'm making you *wait* in this awful way," she dithered, scudding across to a trestle table at the far end of the room, where she began scrabbling furiously in the sprawl of

papers. "It's called 'Hugh Tatnall: The Rhetoric of Inattention,' I can't imagine why, it's not about literature at all, oh
where *is* the thing!" she babbled, loose papers flying. "Anyway
this professor who wrote it just doesn't know *anything* about
how Hugh worked, Professor Shipley, and why he picked on
Piranesi of *all* poss— Oh here it is!" she cried blissfully. "I
mean it's not a *real* research project for me, it's just about this
one series of Hugh's sketches and I still have to check years of
bibliography, he did them way back in 1940, I wasn't even
born! But this morning I've been working and I've *proved*
how utterly this professor's interpretation— *Would* you like to
look at what I've done?" she murmured, eyes like great stars
at me. "While I dress? Would you I mean really, because I
won't be two minutes if you would"—thrust her discoveries at
me with a warm little hand, and was gone again.

The top sheet seemed to be some sort of mistake: it was
blank except for a mimeographed

7. "The progression from a realistic to a symbolic mode is
recapitulated on a level of consciousness where the mode in
which meaning is created becomes itself a special part of the
meaning."—Discuss, with reference to any *two* decades since 1900.

Ah, well, English departments go down flags flying. I turned
the sheet over, and politely began to read.

The phone rang.

"What are you doing?"

I said, " 'Doing'?"

"Sweetie you haven't rung me up for half an hour!"

"I was supposed to?"

"Well but by *this* time, goodness, shouldn't you have got
started back with her?"

"She'll be dressed any minute."

" '*Be* dressed'?"

"She had a learned morning. Did a research paper."

"*Naked?*"

"Or whatever it is girls don't wear when they don't wear it."

"But sweetie the morning of Hugh's *funeral?*"

"Smith girls are serious-minded. We inculcate it. This one's just more inculcated than you're used to."

"What are you talking about?"

"Anyway she's been engaged to a Yale boy all year—serious-mindedness itself."

"Engaged when she was with *Hugh?*"

"Total fidelity. Said to me in Florence, 'Why, Professor Shipley, I write to him every day.'"

The phone was speechless.

So I said, "You don't realize the hair-raising conduct you can confront us with. Not that I understand it either. Merely that with each one of you my ignorance is enriched with additional incomprehensions."

A faintly smiling silence. Then she said, "You tell us you love us and we tell you we love you and really it's a darling metaphor. Or good manners. What one's taught to say. And taught one feels. But *in love* must be a madness."

Silence again. I was still decoding when she went on from whatever it was, "Sweet Simon this *won't* last."

"That make it any the less an enchantment?"

"So you do know that."

"If you'd thought I didn't it wouldn't have happened."

"And you're trying to keep my resistance melted by reminding me that it did?"

"Yes."

"How lucky nothing's so simple as you like to make it sound," she said sweetly, and hung up; and I went back to Persis's research.

The child took more than her two minutes. Or than her earlier five. But the eventual result was a properly seductive production, eyes demure, lips murmuring their penitence, and all aimed at me, so I said how admirably entertained her paper had kept me.

"Oh *do* you like it, Professor Shipley?" she cried, instantly beaming.

I said why on earth not?—if she was as hard-working as this she'd graduate next year with a magna. And obligingly added, nothing against being smart as well as beautiful, so suddenly there she was all dimples at me.

Priorities are however priorities. I said did she want to gather up these papers of hers? because we ought to be starting for the meetinghouse—and, by the way, didn't she still have some sketches of Hugh's too?

A stricken silence.

I said, trying to sound kindly or whatever, I meant that series she'd been the model for.

She looked at me in misery, swallowing.

"Because you do have them, don't you," I said.

"Oh how can I make you understand!" she cried, wretchedly. "I didn't take them to *have*, Professor Shipley, I mean like keepsakes, I only took them to protect his— He was a *wonderful* painter, everything he did had always— But *these* were only some very preliminary sketches for a madonna, I mean just sort of *parts* of me, like my, well, my legs in a lot of different trial poses, and my b-bosom, and the *trouble* was, Professor Shipley, that when I tried to find out why he was planning a *nude* madonna he just laughed at me! Till I was in tears! I felt like, well, you know all those girls of Cellini's in his autobiography?—why, except for that Caterina in Paris, when he was working for François I, Cellini doesn't even mention their names! And they'd *had babies* by him! And then one night we made love twice, and again in the morning, and he started the real composition—and it was the next day that Francesca killed him. And all that was left were *pieces* of me. And then you arrived and I—I— Well, I hid the sketches and everything from you because *all* they would do was mock his reputation," she sniffled. "I don't mean I'm a critic or anything but I couldn't bear to have people see them and *find out* how Hugh— Oh, he was so *valuable*, Professor Shipley, oh *do* you see what I mean about it all?" she choked, and by this time she naturally turned out to be more or less in my arms.

So then she wept there briefly.

But in due course we dried her tears; she scudded off to do her face over; we collected her suitcases; she scribbled a note to her adviser; we proceeded to the car; she raced back for another suitcase; we stowed it with the others in the trunk; she murmured as if in caress "Do you think I'm awful?" I said "Only in principle"; and off we went, into the warm annunciations of noon.

Presently, as we drove, she said dreamily, "Have you always had someone in love with you, Professor Shipley?"

I said hardly a question a man would have the want of punctilio and gratitude to answer No to.

"Oh it is so nice, isn't it!" she cried. "And *necessary*, when you're a girl! Otherwise you feel so discouraged."

Ah, well, I said, there were these vapors, these special declines her sex felt called upon to go into over ours. Whereas if the ordinary male didn't get his young woman after being led some outrageous dallying chase for weeks on end, heavily out of pocket perhaps too, did *he* repine?

"Oh, I *know* about Hugh's girls," she said slightingly, as if this were a reply, and went into a reverie.

After a time she said, in a brooding voice, "Sometimes, *now*, I can't decide whether I was *in* love with Profess—with Hugh, Professor Shipley. Maybe I just sort of wanted to own him. Or d'you think? Of course I had this—I suppose it was romantic, what would it be like, living with him and making love and having him wild about me, and I got him to let me sit in on his senior seminar and then, well, there *I* was in Italy! Oh the things that happen to you are so accidental somehow, aren't they, it doesn't look as if anybody ever planned anything very much at all, does it! I don't know if it was what I'd expected, sort of. I don't mean I was disappointed, I was *living* with him, and he was wonderful, but I was just so surprised sometimes. Maybe because I've never lived like *that* with anybody, or d'you think," she said uneasily. "Because there can be this loneliness in being *with* somebody too. I mean he wanted me *there*, and he got very grim about Francesca, but did he think I was *me*—me, Persis—what I am, I mean? So how am I to know about anything!" she burst out, gazing at me with great softly accusing eyes.

And back into her reverie.

Till in fact we reached Camilla's. Who greeted me with a bland "Why, it's you! You got her clothes back on her again and *got* her here? sweetie how resourceful," and off we drove to the funeral.

I X

> Sur tant de portes tant de clefs
> Le long des couloirs de ton âme

What mistaken conclusions was I to decide to come to here, then, about my lifelong friend and fellow-man, before these interminable Quakers called it an hour? What misgaugings or misjudgings or·misinterpretations? What simple oversights? What imaginary truths altogether?

A classicist is trained to suspect (and a few of us do) that much of what we know is misinformation, and much of what isn't is beyond sensible explanation anyhow. If an archaeologist finds Linear B scribblings on, say, fragments of an Attic black-figure amphora, what conclusions is he to arrive at?— rewrite the complete chronology of the ancient Ægean still a twentieth time? Suppose Hugh an archaeological scavo, then: how am I to account for such total unexpectednesses as that

drawerful of mementos? No trained classicist would maintain
that I had, as the phrase is, "seen him without illusions." He
had blandly presented me with alternative illusions I could see
him under instead, and the historical "truth" was beyond even
hypothesis.

And think of the assorted illusions of the world at large!
The man in the street thought of Hugh's paintings, if he
thought of them at all, as simulacra; the academic establishment saw them, with equal absurdity, as symbols. And his
behavior as metaphor. Hugh as Hugh had vanished into a haze
of myth long since. Painters I admit are a libertine, arrogant,
lawless, and singularly inarticulate lot; they do exhibit, and
without explanation, what Aragon called "le goût du saccage."
But the stereotype is delusory: any "taste for havoc" that
describes, say, Gauguin or van Gogh is obviously neither here
nor there about Cézanne or Degas.

Nor did stereotypes explain even the libertine side of Hugh.
The mutual incompetences of our mating habits are immemorial, and even the expertise of Ovid could be baffled:

Cur mihi *plus aequo* flavi placuêre capilli?

—"Why did that golden head *so immoderately* delight me? . . ."
But only a sad sociologist would quantify Hugh's fluttering
amies de rechange as Case Studies In Ladylike Nonsense. Perhaps Hugh's old uncle had unconsciously taught him, but he
took a pleasure in the ballet of coquetry that most men seem
never to suspect is there, the fascination of waiting for this or
that sweetly dallying girl to show you what situation, and what
style, she has imagined for handing herself over in; and
whether it was in fact this or Hugh himself they loved, the
covenant had a humaneness it would never have occurred to a
simple libertine was what in fact made the pleasure a pleasure.
Often they found themselves moved simply by how moved
they were; or that nightlong in a lover's arms they can lie

entranced discussing themselves as an Episode, as an Epiphany, in a dialogue of recited mementos, delighted with themselves—and hence with him.

—But here now at the end, I said to myself, the secret essence of him gone, I wish there had been someone with a less disenchanted, a kindlier, intelligence than Taige's or mine to have said what was said, of a friend as much like a brother as one is ever likely to share the intractable farrago of a lifetime with. As my fellow-man he was a fellow-marauder, but I assessed his performance with I hope a disabused impartiality, noting his methods as I did any other male's. If, like any other male's, I sometimes found them surprising, this was perhaps an inevitable vanity. For though I had known him from our boyhood, one has always to remember the Dryden—

> Farewell, too nigh me, too familiar grown,
> To think thy nature, as thine image, known.

Nor is the artist ever Man writ large. Make him over to the specifications of humanity and you have upset the ecology of creativity. So let us unmoralize. The secret essence within is gone.

—At which point, as if I had said it aloud and been heard with approval, the grave overseers facing the meeting rose and shook hands with each other and with Taige: the hour was up. We rose, and began working our several ways along the lines of ancient benches toward the aisles and the doors.

Except that I heard a whispered "Professor Shipley?" and found Persis looking up at me starry-eyed.

"Oh Professor Shipley," she breathed, "*would* it d'you think be all right if I went up and told Professor Heald—I mean what he said was *so* perfect! Could I just I mean tell him how wonderful I thought he was? . . ."

Well, she was of age. "My guess is," I said in my kindliest tone, "he'd be charmed."

"Oh Professor *Shipley*," she sighed to me, and was gone, as single-mindedly straight for Taige as a bee for nectar.

"But shouldn't you have told her to write her daily letter to her Yale boy first?" said Camilla.

I said now now, hadn't she at least a spectator's indulgence watching the logistics of an agreeable future take shape? and slowly we drifted on toward the doors.

On and out, in our dozens and scores, into the blandishments of noon. An amiable learned nattering rose around us: we might, in our groups, have been issuing from the genialities and backbitings of a faculty meeting, the agenda of the spirit dealt with, minds in order, disbursed, and at ease. "And anyway," Camilla murmured as we sauntered away, "immortality's so reassuring to hear about—other people's especially."

But it was the low assurances of mortal things that I found my mind was on, and I said, "Are you going to be an angel of angels?"

". . . and do what?"

"Have for instance lunch with me?"

"I make you hungry too? goodness how gratifying!"

"All I thought was—"

"Or did you just mean 'lunch first'?"

"God help me," I said, "what can a man do with a woman he's out of his mind over, but offer her any excuse he can think of for doing what he helplessly hopes she'll do no matter what he says?"

"Oh sweetie are you charming me again?"

"You don't feel you know?"

"Ah Simon who are you and I to suppose it of ourselves that we *examine* what we do with our feelings? . . ."

"You couldn't give it a lovely try?"

"Sweet Simon," she said, sliding a gloved hand through my arm, "you can't *still* be surprised!"

So, as I recall it, I answered, "Always"—enchantment being (with luck) what it can sometimes turn out to be.